D0790926

BLOOD FIGHT

To Wayland Jarrett's surprise, the Montana cattle buyer suddenly spurred his paint horse forward into a fast canter. Puzzling over this, Jarrett glanced up at the rocky heights. In the drawn-black darkness of the moonlit night, he couldn't make out any movement. At his back, just the sounds of his trail crew riding behind him. Then it came all at once — muzzle flashes from both sides of the small meadow and the throaty varooming of rifles.

Jarrett was one of the first to be hit, but somehow he held his saddle, a man confused but still managing to claw out his sidearm. Only their wasn't anything to shoot at. He got as far as the thorny bushes hedging the meadow when one of the ambushers let go a slug that tore into his lower back. Jarrett's horse started to pitch and buck and rag doll him away. He didn't remember falling into the thorns of a large bush as everything went black.

ZEBRA'S HEADING WEST!

with GILES, LEGG, PARKINSON, LAKE, KAMMEN, and MANNING

KANSAS TRAIL   (3517, $3.50/$4.50)
by Hascal Giles
After the Civil War ruined his life, Bennett Kell threw in his lot with a gang of thievin' guntoughs who rode the Texas-Kansas border. But there was one thing he couldn't steal—fact was, Ada McKittridge had stolen his heart.

GUNFIGHT IN MESCALITO   (3601, $3.50/$4.50)
by John Legg
Jubal Crockett was a young man with a bright future—until that Mescalito jury found him guilty of murder and sentenced him to hang. Jubal'd been railroaded good and the only writ of habeus corpus was a stolen key to the jailhouse door and a fast horse!

DRIFTER'S LUCK   (3396, $3.95/$4.95)
by Dan Parkinson
Byron Stillwell was a drifter who never went lookin' for trouble, but trouble always had a way of findin' him. Like the time he set that little fire up near Kansas to head off a rogue herd owned by a cattle baron named Dawes. Now Dawes figures Stillwell owes him something . . . at the least, his life.

MOUNTAIN MAN'S VENGEANCE   (3619, $3.50/$4.50)
by Robert Lake
The high, rugged mountain made John Henry Trapp happy. But then a pack of gunsels thundered across his land, burned his hut, and murdered his squaw woman. Trapp hit the vengeance trail and ended up in jail. Now he's back and how that mountain has changed!

BIG HORN HELLRIDERS   (3449, $3.50/$4.50)
by Robert Kammen
Wyoming was a tough land and toughness was required to tame it. Reporter Jim Haskins knew the Wyoming tinderbox was about to explode but he didn't know he was about to be thrown smack-dab in the middle of one of the bloodiest range wars ever.

TEXAS BLOOD KILL   (3577, $3.50/$4.50)
by Jason Manning
Ol' Ma Foley and her band of outlaw sons were cold killers and most folks in Shelby County, Texas knew it. But Federal Marshal Jim Gantry was no local lawman and he had his guns cocked and ready when he rode into town with one of the Foley boys as his prisoner.

Available wherever paperbacks are sold, or order direct from the Publisher. Send cover price plus 50¢ per copy for mailing and handling to Zebra Books, Dept. 4033, 475 Park Avenue South, New York, N.Y. 10016. Residents of New York and Tennessee must include sales tax. DO NOT SEND CASH. For a free Zebra/ Pinnacle catalog please write to the above address.

ROBERT KAMMEN

RATTLERS ROOST

ZEBRA BOOKS
KENSINGTON PUBLISHING CORP.

ZEBRA BOOKS

are published by

Kensington Publishing Corp.
475 Park Avenue South
New York, NY 10016

Copyright © 1993 by Robert Kammen

All rights reserved. No part of this book may be reproduced in any form or by any means without the prior written consent of the Publisher, excepting brief quotes used in reviews.

Zebra and the Z logo are trademarks of Kensington Publishing Corp.

If you purchased this book without a cover you should be aware that this book is stolen property. It was reported as "unsold and destroyed" to the Publisher and neither the Author nor the Publisher has received any payment for this "stripped book."

First Printing: January, 1993

Printed in the United States of America

Prologue

For Guy Jarrett it was the terrible agony of not knowing if Reba Jo or the rest of them were still alive. A few missing cattle could be explained away, a man misplacing some saddle gear, and sometimes lonely cowhands riding their broncs into sinkholes and never seen again. But a trail herd of some two thousand cattle just up and disappearing. Along with the men bringing them up from Texas. And all a man had to go on was a letter postmarked out of Sheridan, Wyoming.

Snow showers had hindered Guy Jarrett's passage up along the Little Bighorn for most of the day, a bitterly cold day in late February of 1889, though the winter had been a lot milder than those of three years ago. Then, in a bitter rampage, blizzards had wiped out herds from the Dakotas clear down into Texas. Ranchers he'd known for years simply gave up, with hard times the order of the day for both cattleman and cowtown.

Salvation of a sort were advertisements placed in local newspapers by the Divide Cattle Company out of Montana. All a rancher had to do to get top dollar for his cattle was to trail herd them up to the

5

copper camp at Butte, as thereabouts it was boom-time. A far piece to trail a herd, according to some of Guy Jarrett's neighbors, but it was the only way any of them could hold onto their ranches. The middle of last February saw Guy Jarrett and his brother, Wayland, throwing in their Circle J-J cattle with herds belonging to Micah Cade and Sid Holt. From here on the plan was to travel with the grass, a legacy of the old and great trail herds. The only thing was, instead of heading out as trail boss, rancher Guy Jarrett found himself exchanging his saddle for a hospital bed.

Guy's vow to catch up with the herd never came about due to peritonitis setting in following an appendicitis operation. For a while it was touch and go, his body wasting away as the infection spread throughout his stomach cavity, and most of Guy Jarrett's thoughts were on the woman who'd gone with the herd. Out of the hospital at last, he took a buggy out to his ranch to recuperate, his spirits lifted one day by a letter sent from up in Oklahoma by Reba Jo Cade. It spoke of the hardships of the trail, chiefly of how much Reba Jo loved him. A second letter came from Colorado, and had Guy chafing to throw a saddle onto his claybank and head it northerly.

When Guy Jarrett finally made up his mind to head out, and with him still gaunt and not fully recovered, 1889 had about run its course. He knew they should have been back before this, a couple of months at least. A final letter had come, the one he was now packing in a buttoned-down shirt pocket. But as trail boss his brother, Wayland, should have sent a message from the end-of-the-line-town, Butte, Montana.

"In weather like this," rasped out Guy Jarrett, "I

can see them losing a few head. But they got up there in midsummer."

The snowfall thickened to drape away the low-humping Rosebuds off to Guy's right. He'd tied his hat down to keep his ears from frostbite, rode hunkered up in a sheepskin on a vague trail—the snow on it slushy wet but thickening. Alongside the trail in silent companionship flowed a river known to all westerners. Pan ice clung along the banks of the Little Bighorn, its waters up now in warming weather that had caused some snowmelt. Every so often the formless gray clouds seemed to lighten up but still the snow fell in big soggy drops. Off his left shoulder he could make out that the Bighorns weren't as high, while back some ten miles lay a waystop called Wyola.

This passageway was also part of the bloody Bozeman Trail, as Guy recalled. Scarcely two decades ago miners ventured through there on their way to the mining camps of Virginia City and Helena. Later on it was settlers, and on into the 1880s, the trail herds. From what he'd learned recently back at Sheridan this portion of the trail passed through the Crow Reservation.

"At least the Crow sided with the cavalry," Guy murmured edgily. Throughout the snow-dusted day, by his reckonings, drawing onto late afternoon, he had yet to encounter another traveler. Weather such as this favored hostiles or men riding the high lines. Ahead not all that far should be Lodge Grass, and where he was hoping to spend the night.

Harking back to less'n a month ago and his inquiries in Denver, Guy found out that some trail herds had passed by that mile-high city. It was from there that Reba Jo had written, some of how she missed him, the rest a narrative of their being met by an agent from the Divide Cattle Company, afterward to push on. Disturbing to Guy Jarrett was that nobody around Denver had ever heard of this particular cattle company.

"Dunwoody, that was it," threw out Guy, his voice muffled by the wind suddenly lashing out. He ducked his head away from an onslaught of snow as the claybank nickered its displeasure. In this weather he knew better than to pick up the gait of his bronc. Lodge Grass; had to be coming up soon.

Neal Dunwoody had been one of a pair of cattle buyers who came down to roam through western Texas, and as Guy remembered now, kind of gracious when it came to buying drinks around. Texas newspapers had bonafided Dunwoody's story that Butte was a boomtown. The cattle buyer had even grubstaked some ranchers to supplies and a little cash so's they could make a drive.

Here the trail had narrowed in between naked trees and pines, their branches sagging under the weight of wet snow, and the river was closer, so that when the bronc stumbled, for a moment Guy thought it had slipped over the high bank. This caused him to tip forward, and to have his weight settle against the forks of his saddle. Reining up, he realized the range of what he could see had closed in considerable: that the snow was slanting in more because of the wind picking up. And something else, that across the river a light was flickering beneath a basseting of cliff rock and deep among a brûlée of dead trees and brush. Probably another traveler like him, but to get there would mean having to ford the Little Bighorn.

Hesitation rode an uncertain trail across Guy's leather-cheeked face. Soggy snow was draping to wet his outer garments and as it hit it melted, to seep through the cracks in his clothes, and he knew the claybank would also welcome a chance to get out of this weather. He spurred the bronc on, as it seemed all of a sudden that it had gotten a lot darker as if a man had doused a lamp. Soon he came to a wider section of river, where a sandbar lay exposed close to midstream. With some reluctance the claybank came down the low bank and splashed into the river, and with Guy's fear that the bottom might be quicksandy. But he made it across without incident, leaving cross-ripples in the wake of his bronc.

Now he cut back along the east bank to where he'd last seen that campfire. There was barely enough passage for the bronc through the branches of firs shoving aside, and upon spotting the fire barely discernible in the dark thickness of the brûlée, he reined up to call out,

"Hello, the fire!"

The claybank sensed a presence first, and it took a couple of hopping steps forward, and then Guy heard the crunching of snow from just behind. Slowly, as a man wanting nothing more than to get rid of a kink in his back he raised his arms, and said, "Your campfire looked awful inviting, mister."

Stepping into the open came an Indian swaddled up in buckskin, who motioned with his carbine for Guy to dismount. And as he did, the rancher from Texas saw there were two of them, and he shaped a friendly smile.

The one in buckskins said gutturally, "Had you been a Northern Cheyenne . . ." He turned with a disdainful abruptness and ghosted back in through the shabby lay of fallen trees and the standing pines, to have his companion jab out with the barrel of his carbine.

"Okay," said Guy Jarrett in response. He brought his horse in followed by who he figured was a Crow Indian. The sheltering timber cut away the force of the snowfall and wind, and then he came onto a shelter cave recessed into the base of the sheer cliff wall. Squatting by the fire and wrapped up in an Indian blanket so that only his low-crowned hat showed was another Crow, and just the three of them according to the horses tethered nearby.

"A strange brand?"

Guy blinked at the Crow snuckered in by the campfire as he'd spoken in fluent English, and Guy's response was, "Just rode up from Texas. My claybank's plumb tuckered out from fightin' this snow . . . same's me. I'm Guy Jarrett. That venison smells mighty tangy."

"There is enough for all."

Nodding, Guy brought his bronc past the campfire, where he tied the reins to a branch before removing the saddle. He used the saddle blanket to wipe some of the wet snow away from the shoulders and flanks of his horse, and in doing so, kept casting testing eyes at the Indians settling in around the campfire. "There, get acquainted with these cayuses." And turning away, Guy held onto his saddle blanket as he bent over to open a saddlebag and take out a tin cup. He stepped over to the campfire to have low-crowned hat say,

"To my Crow brothers I am Black Feather. But to a lot of settlers coming in I'm called a nuisance. It seems your white brothers, Mr. Jarrett, want our lands."

"You go to a mission school . . ."

"Yes, not all that far away" Black Feather made a vague hand gesture and continued, "St. Xavier."

Guy held out his cup as a black pot was brought

10

his way, to have black coffee spill into it. The ambered eyes of the Crow holding it were as unreadable as a puma's. Though Black Feather seemed to be unarmed, both of the other Crow had their long guns close at hand, one of them an army carbine with brass tacks patterning the wooden stock. The coffee, he found, was acrid and scalding to his stomach, but it chased a lot of chill away.

"What brings you out in this weather?" he said, as he set down his cup and started to unbutton his sheepskin with leather-gloved hands.

Another vague hand gesture came from Black Feather along with a smile that lifted the corners of his wide mouth. "Horse thiefs; the ancient trade still goes on. Only now instead of killing Northern Cheyenne we turn them over to the law. Sometimes" . . . now his eyes smiled, too . . . "we forget."

A word from one of the other Crow cut away the exchange of words as he slashed away with his hunting knife at the large hunk of roasted venison. Before joining in, Guy removed his gloves, and then held out his hands to warm them over the flames. The ring on his left hand caught their attention, one he'd had specially-made down at Ciudad Juarez in Old Mexico. It was of abalone pearl, a hololith made from a single piece of gem material, pale-green and shining some in the light of the fire. From the same piece of abalone pearl had come a necklace presented to the woman he was to marry. All at once he felt bone weary, and a lot older than thirty-five. *Reba Jo; damn woman, just where in tarnation are you?*

As his companions started a low monologue in Crow about possessing such a ring, Black Feather shrugged the blanket aside revealing his outer gar-

11

ment was of elkskin. He was stocky with a square head; his braided hair coming over his shoulders. He chewed away quietly, studying covertly the lean and russet-haired Texan. The gun he saw under the folds of the coat told him a lot, as it was a .44 single-action Colt's with a blue steel barrel and a worn plain cedar stock, which to Black Feather meant that it had seen much use. The face was interesting too, stubbled with maybe a three-day's growth of beard, the skin wind-scoured over the angular shape of the white man's face, the light blue eyes at once friendly yet alert to everything that was happening, the changing voice of the passing snow shower, and close at hand. A dangerous adversary, pondered the Crow, yet there was more. This Guy Jarrett didn't have the look of a man on the dodge, rather of someone seeking to solve a mystery. He sensed further that Jarrett would speak in due course, so Black Feather went back to the business of enjoying the venison.

"How much farther to Lodge Grass?"

The passage of about twenty minutes had come before that question from Guy Jarrett knifed across the campfire, and in response Black Feather said, "Perhaps two miles."

A shrugging grin from Guy was followed by, "Could make that easy enough. But . . . this seems a nice spot to spend the night . . ."

"My friends, Deer That Runs and Wolf Killer, speak of how they want your ring, Jarrett. Do you still wish to tarry here for the night?"

"You've got trustful eyes, Black Feather."

"But perhaps a black heart." The Crow laughed, whereupon he spoke in his own tongue to the others. Among the Crow was a low exchange of words, to which Black Feather added, "They will

12

hear you out, Jarrett."

"Hear me out?"

"It is as plain to the Crow as that horned owl sheltered in yonder tree that something bad has touched your heart. When you looked at your ring, Jarrett, your soul came to stand naked in your eyes. Only a woman can bring out such naked pain."

"By chance, are you a Crow shaman? But you're partly right, Black Feather. I expect some trail herds have passed through your neck of the woods, heading for the copper camp over to Butte and other places up here."

"Last summer a few herds came through. Of course, the Crow exacted a tribute from each one; just a few cattle to help feed our people. This woman . . ."

"Name's Reba Jo Cade—fixin' to marry her, or was." He went on to tell of how most of the cattle he owned were part of a larger herd heading for Butte. He tipped his hat back and stared away for a moment. "Anyways, last word I got was a letter mailed out of Sheridan. Beyond that not even a whisper."

Grimacing, Black Feather exchanged glances with the other Crow, with a nod from him giving voice to Deer That Runs, whose lengthy tirade was accompanied by a lot of hand gestures.

"So, what Deer That Runs spoke of was of evil things happening beyond our lands. To the west, Jarrett. During the summer last year when the herds came through. Gunfire was heard in the breaks north of Crown Butte. As my people were out hunting for game and not white man's trouble they kept away. But as their hunt took them farther to the west, they came upon land chewed up by a passing herd of many, many cattle . . . and something else,

13

Jarrett . . ."

An ember crackling out of the fire caused Guy Jarrett to blink, but he couldn't blink away the fear beginning to stab at his stomach.

"My people came upon a white man hiding in deep thickets. This man's clothes were all torn . . . and blood stained his face. As blood should, since one eye had been gouged out. He had been shot in the lower back . . . but that is not all, Jarrett. His mind had snapped, so that he could not tell my people what happened."

"My . . . God." Guy ran a trembling hand along his temple.

"They have him now, the priests of St. Xavier's. They keep him locked in a cabin."

"What about the cattle, the others?"

Shrugging, Black Feather said quietly, "Gone; only the Great Spirit knows where."

"How far is it to the mission . . . ?"

"A morning's ride. In the morning we will take you there."

This promise was kept by Black Feather, the Crow leaving Guy Jarrett on a lonely hillock a short distance away from a scattering of buildings marked by the spire of a church.

The sky had cleared, and the temperature was warming into the fifties. As for last night, though Guy had snugged up in his bedroll, all he caught were brief moments of sleep. And not because he feared the Crow would make a go for his ring, but the dread of what was to come when he arrived at the mission; that it would be someone he knew. A reluctant spur brought the claybank loping down the gentle slope, wisps of clouds sweeping low over the distant Bighorns.

Coming in amongst the buildings, he passed a

14

few Indians loafing before a large log building as a robed priest came out. Reining up, Guy swung down as the priest said,

"That's a Texas saddle."

"Yup, it be that."

"So, my son, I'm Father Mulcahey." He extended a work-worn hand.

"Guy Jarrett. Reason I'm here, sir, is that yesterday, or more like last night, I ran into some Crow. South along the Little Bighorn."

"It is obvious, Mr. Jarrett, they told you about one of our guests. Obviously a cowhand, too." He gestured to bring one of the Indians over. "He'll tend to your horse, Mr. Jarrett. Come, come this way."

"Maybe my brother brought the herd through here?"

"Generally, Mr. Jarrett, they stick to the river. Up north the Northern Pacific has holding pens along its mainline. I gather just outside of Billings." They passed the log church, beyond which lay a log cabin with barred windows. As they cleared the shadow of the church, the priest slowed his pace and said, "We don't know this man's name . . . and strangely enough when he was brought here he carried no wallet or other papers. For a while it was touch and go, Mr. Jarrett. Somehow the good Lord has decreed that he live. And somehow . . ." The eyes of Father Mulcahey held a quizzical look. "He's older than you . . . but . . ."

At last they stood before the locked cabin door, and it took considerable willpower for Guy Jarrett not to rip the keys out of the priest's hands and unlock the door. Removing the lock, the priest eased the door open and glanced inside, then he motioned Guy after him. The one-room cabin contained just a barren table and chair and a wooden bunk. A vague form balled up in a fetal position huddled against the west wall.

As yet, Guy couldn't make out who it was, and he found himself whispering, "Can't make out his face."

"We call him Johnny, for want of a name. Go in carefully, Mr. Jarrett, as Johnny does resort to violence at times."

Doffing his Stetson, Guy set it on the table. A couple of cautious steps brought him over to the wall, where he bent over and reached out a tentative hand. The attire worn by the one called Johnny was an old brown cowl, the hood up over his head, and now he flopped around to cringe away from the man bending over him, a harsh, animal-like scream coming out of his mouth. Only one eye had been gouged out, and though a livid scar bridged across the other eye, he could still see out of it. The rest of the face was a thin, pale mask stretched over bone.

The wind sucked out of Guy Jarrett's lungs, all he could do was to hold there and stare down at his only brother, Wayland. "He's . . . Father . . . he's . . ."

"Been that way, son, ever since he was brought here. I'm afraid he'll never come out of it. You do know him."

"Wayland," rasped Guy, "my brother, Wayland." He couldn't tear his eyes away from his brother who started to tremble more, with spittle trickling out of the corners of his mouth. Now in the aftershock of finding Wayland he remembered there were others. He wanted to embrace his brother, found that he couldn't, discovered also as he turned away that an anger had settled in.

16

"Come, Mr. Jarrett," the priest said regretfully. "We can go to my office and talk about this."

Then an animal scream pierced out at Guy. He half-turned, the next moment to have Wayland Jarrett come flailing at him. Somehow he evaded the weak blows of his brother and wrapped his arms around Wayland's torso. "Easy, Wayland," he called out as his eyes began misting in the horror of all of this, and as the fight went out of the man he held, Guy Jarrett held on tighter, murmuring, "Its me, Way, your kin . . . please . . . try to understand . . ."

He managed to guide his brother over to lower him onto the bed, and now reluctant to let go, and seeing no spark of recognition nor remembrance of what had happened in Wayland Jarrett's eye staring blankly back at him. As if he was alone, the man the priests called Johnny turned to work himself into a fetal position of forgetfulness and away from Guy Jarrett.

Guy found himself leaving ahead of Father Mulcahey, who locked the cabin door. He found himself too numbed of mind to comprehend what he had just seen. Now in a disjointed way the names of those sharing the long trail up from Texas were spoken by Guy Jarrett, "Holt and Butterfield . . . Buddy Keane . . . Reba, Reba Jo . . ."

"Yes, Mr. Jarrett, the shock of it all . . ."

"I . . . I've got to find out what happened, Father Mulcahey."

"It wouldn't be the Crow doing this?"

"Nope, not them." He fell into step with the priest, afraid to glance back at the log cabin, a man drained and just groping along. "I reckon I've got to push on, to the railhead up at Billings. If they

17

got that far. My brother, Way, I'll . . ."

"We'll be your brother's keeper for now, Mr Jarrett."

"Before, padre, it was always Way looking out for me. But it'll be white men I'm after."

"We'll be praying for you, Mr. Jarrett."

Harshly, Guy Jarrett retorted, "You'd better include those who did this in your prayers, padre."

Guy Jarrett left within the hour, a man changed forever by the awful revelation he'd discovered back at St. Xavier's Mission. He'd left with those men of the cloth his hot, harsh words to exact vengeance. He never looked back.

Chapter One

Habit ingrained from countless nights such as this brought wagon boss Ira Hembree snail-pacing away from the campfire to pass alongside the chuck wagon. Away from the glare of the fire he tipped his head back, held his eyes to the northern sky as he tried to fix in on the polestar. Vaguely he became aware of someone soft-footing in behind him, knew without bothering to look it would be Reba Jo Cade. Gumming his upper plate around, Hembree said,

"Reckon there'll be no need to follow the tongue anymore. Not with them Bighorns behind us." It had been a nightly ritual of pointing the tongue of the chuck wagon toward the polestar. And then he located the star beaming out of a pitch black sky. "Like an old friend."

"Marks true north does the North Star."

He swung around in an awkward shuffle, a scraggly-bearded man, hatless, and clad in an old gray shirt and soiled trousers. The respect he held for Reba Jo shone in his eyes. Among other things was his learning of her being a school teacher once upon a long ago time. That after her mother had passed away, Reba Jo had re-

19

turned to the Cade Ranch to help out her father. Ten years later she was still awful pretty, he felt, and would make a good woman for Guy Jarrett still back in Texas.

"Yup, Reba Jo, learned a lot about this high heaven of the Almighty's from you. A long haul up here to Montana, too. But, Lordy, the stars will be out tonight."

"Another week before we pull into Billings, according to Wayland."

"In a way, I hate to see it." Scratching at his beard, he looked skyward. "Let's see now . . . them's the two tail stars of Ursa Minor . . . an' that's Charles's Wain . . . and that one . . ."

"The Plough, Ira. Just follow them for some five times their distance apart, and—"

"Be eying the polestar, I reckon."

Reba Jo Cade gazed westerly where the last chaffs of reddish hue tinted the horizon ridged by distant mountains. Opposite a few miles lay a watery obstacle, the Bighorn River, etching down through the heart of the Crow Indian Reservation. Tribute in the form of two steers had been paid to the Crow, and once they cleared the reservation the last barrier between here and Billings was Pryor Creek.

"Another three, four days," she murmured in turning to follow after Hembree.

Ira Hembree, using his apron tail to lift the lid on the kettle wedged over the fire, muttered dryly, "You don't sound all that happy, Miss Cade."

"Oh, I'm glad it's about over." She picked out a tin cup from an assortment of silverware in a wash pan and helped herself to coffee. "Just worried about Guy."

20

"Guy's tougher'n whangleather. But you know, Miss Cade, your betrothed did like to go down to Old Mexico a lot to visit them señoritas."

"Ha, Mr. Hembree," she laughed, "you've been trying to get my goat all the way up here."

"Got it, too, at times, I reckon. Taters are still harder'n bottom rock. A little more salt won't hurt neither."

As he shuffled around and reached into the cupboard built into the back of the chuck wagon, Reba Jo took a few pensive steps to hold up at the fringe of light spilling out from the fire. Heading in from the herd ground, placed this evening on a huge meadow, were four riders. While the cattle were a darker mass behind the approaching horsemen, here and there the hatted silhouettes kept watch over the herd. About half a year viewing this same scene was something that had gotten to her, brought them closer as of a family, and for sure she'd miss it.

As for Reba Jo Cade, she would be the first to admit that holding to the saddle every day was at first almost unbearable. Likewise had been getting used to a bedroll, and a sky for a roof. Somehow she'd endured. Even when wanting so desperately to rein her bronc around and head back to Texas and the man she loved.

This almost happened down when they were nearly into Colorado. It was a day when massive hammerhead clouds seemed to be chasing after Ira Hembree heading into the cowtown of Cruze to buy supplies, with Reba Jo going along to help out. As the clouds jostled closer, thunderclaps pealed out a warning to expect rain, which came just after Hembree and Reba Jo Cade made it

21

into Cruze. And there in Brewster's Mercantile Exchange while Hembree was going over his list of supplies with the storekeeper, Reba Jo had sidled up to a full-length mirror to check out what the hardships of the trail had done to her.

The woman staring back at her in the reflecting glass of the mirror couldn't possibly be the daughter of Micah Cade. The eyes with the green of new cottonwood leaves were too self-assured. As for the full and curving lips, there were a few cracks in them caused by wind and sun, and matched up well with the tanned face. Most surprising at that moment was the willowy figure encased in Levi's and vest and long-sleeved shirt, as though she was twenty again. But the woman turning away from the mirror was a thirtyish Reba Jo Cade, and realizing that every day was taking them farther and farther from Guy Jarrett.

"Almost did go back," Reba Jo said over the rim of her cup as she watched her father and others removing the saddles from their horses. "But here we are in Montana, at long last." She reached up under the collar of her shirt and spilled out the abalone pearl necklace, the touch of it lifting her spirits. "Love you, Guy."

Approaching in step with Wayland Jarrett, both of them grinning about something, Micah Cade doffed his big-brimmed hat. Above the creaseline the hat had made in his forehead whitish skin rode up to iron-gray hair plastered to his skull. He wasn't as tall as Jarrett, but was big-boned and Micah Cade had a large head. Cade had married late in life, as was the case with a lot of Westerners, chiefly because out on the high plains good women were few and far between. His vices were few, chawing and a drink now and then, denied his being in his late sixties. No matter the weather Cade always wore a coat, as he considered it undignified to do otherwise. And, no longer did he have any misgivings about Reba Jo going along. An affectionate sparkle in his eye, he drawled to his daughter,

"Ira make that coffee any stronger?"

"I spilled a few drops on the back of my hand and it burned the hair away. That strong enough."

Enjoying the byplay, Wayland Jarrett threw in, "Ira made it thicker'n soup before, Micah. Any stronger an' we can tar the wagon hubs." He caught a glimpse of Reba Jo pushing the necklace she wore under her shirt collar, allowed a teasing grin to reveal bony-white teeth. A month ago he'd turned forty-one, a tall and rangy man and quiet of manner. The crew he bossed called him Way, except for his son, Shad, a gangly sixteen-year-old. They shared a ruddy complexion, and like Reba Jo, Shad Jarrett had come to know the ways of the trail. "I guess Guy isn't the only one chafing at the bit."

"You mooning about him again?" asked Micah Cade. "Lucky for us, Way, Ira's chief cook and bottle washer."

"Just wait you two," she snapped back, "there'll be no church wedding as Guy and me'll just elope."

Micah Cade shook his head in mock anger, "Can you beat that, Way, such disrespect coming from my only child. Here I be, going into my fifties, and my daughter won't honor her ma's dying wish. Yup, this new generation of younkers sure don't respect their elders no more."

"Got the same problem with Shad. Too old to take the whip to 'em; too young to head 'em out on their own."

"Pshaw, you pair of turkey gobblers," said Reba Jo. She stepped toward her father and wrapped an arm around his thick waist, together ambling toward Ira Hembree taking all of this in.

"Heck, Micah, give her a kiss so's we can start chowin' down," Hembree grumbled. "Worked my hands to the bone throwin' this feast together . . ."

"Feast," snorted Micah Cade, "beef and beans washed down with canned peaches. That all they eat over to Sheridan . . ."

"Gotta remember you're in Yankee country," smiled Wayland Jarrett as he held out a tin plate onto which the cook ladled a boiled potato, and from the other kettle gravied beefsteak. "Spare me those beans, Ira."

"Iron—lots of iron in 'em. Keeps a man fit."

"That's what it is?" said Way Jarrett. "Wondered why I had so much trouble gettin' aboard my hoss after chowin' down. Know too, where that clangin' noise came from; my innards, I reckon."

Grabbing a plate, and one for Reba Jo, Micah Cade sidled up to the campfire and said, "Iron in them beans; hoss-shoes, maybe?"

"Pay them no mind, Ira," smiled Reba Jo as she shouldered past her father and held her plate out. "But . . . you could go easy on the beans . . ."

"Complaints, complaints, all I get lately." Ira Hembree's uppers clacked. "Billings, Lordy, what a blessed day that'll be gettin' there."

A canvas awning, poled and pegged down, was attached to the back of the chuck wagon. It was under here that Reba Jo settled with the others on small canvas folding chairs brought along at the insistence of Micah Cade. The other wagon, the calf wagon, held their bedrolls and other rigging. The camp pitched by Ira Hembree was on a rocky elevation occupied by a few sheltering pines. At the base of the rise was thicker grass, and where they'd spread out their bedrolls. Farther along the extra horses of the remuda were holding in a rope corral, though tethered outside were a couple of broncs just ridden in by the pair of cowhands heading for the chuck wagon. While away from the herd ground came others, to leave behind the two waddies standing guard.

The first in was Buddy Keane, a pace behind Felix Armijo, a longtime J-J hand. The smaller of the two, Armijo had big, soulful eyes that never seemed to change expression, and they were almond-colored and just about matching the leather vest he wore over a bright red shirt. They had him pegged as a Mexican, though Reba Jo Cade felt no simple vaquero would speak Castilian Spanish. Her thoughts about this were always parried by Armijo. While Buddy Keane was a moon-faced, take-your-time kind of cowpoke, he'd pick up the pace come payday, getting, as Way Jarrett tabbed it, the payday gait. Keane's money was generally spent on booze and loose women hanging around those west Texas cowtowns. In his cups he was known to profess his undying love to a girl of the cribs and would propose matrimony. Sobering up afterward Buddy Keane couldn't even recall his own name much less what town he chanced to be in. But those he rode with claimed falsely he'd gotten hitched. Then Keane would shy away from that particular cowtown.

"Smells darned good, Ira."

"Fried road apples would smell darned good to you, Buddy boy."

He took in Hembree's retort with a smile, and hitched his belt up over his rotund belly, for Buddy Keane was one of those unable to shake away a lot of body fat. He found a plate and tin cup and fork and came back to the campfire, allowed Felix Armijo to go ahead of him and get his plate filled by Hembree. "Micah," he said, "and you too, Way, I sure do appreciate you letting us check out that Sheridan town."

"See any fillies you like, Buddy?"

"Some. But a man needs more'n one night in a place like that."

"All you'd do, Mr. Keane, is wind up stoned to the gills and probably married again."

"Doggonit, Way, I never did get hitched to none of them Texas . . ." He shot a glance at Reba Jo. "Them Texas ladies."

"Ain't the way we heard it, Buddy." Micah Cade shifted on the folding chair and folded one leg over another, a sign that he was enjoying the exchange. "I'll bet, Mr. Keane, if you was to refresh your memory you'd qualify to join the Mormon Church."

"Here now," Hembree snapped to Keane, "hold that plate steady unless you want these beans poured down the front of your britches."

With a plate rimming with hot food, Buddy Keane moved over to ease down alongside Armijo. He was about to fork into the beans, then held his hand back and looked questioningly at Micah Cade. "Just wha'cha mean, Micah, about me joinin' them Mormons . . . ?"

"Naw," said Way Jarrett, "Buddy couldn't be one of them polygamists. On the other hand, with all them wives of his . . ."

"Prime qualified, I'd say."

Keane's response was to bend to the task of eating. Toward the campground came three more riders. As they approached, Way Jarrett noticed that his son wasn't among them, so he figured Shad had volunteered to stand killpecker guard. He said to Cade, "I like the way those Divide Cattle people have been handling this."

"Treated us damned fine down at Denver. Reckon that bonus money they gave us to finish the drive up at Billings means more in our pockets. Never thought either, Way, that I'd be part of a cattle drive again."

"Our salvation. Hate to think of selling off the horses. Broke in as they are to working cattle. Especially that roan gelding of mine; best cutting hoss I ever had."

The talk trailed off with the arrival of Haw Butterfield, out of the cowtown of Goldsmith, Andy Dovala, and trailing in behind, amiable Kyle Foley. As he started to unbuckle his gunbelt, Butterfield drawled, "Shad talked me into switchin' watches."

Wayland Jarrett nodded his approval.

"Don't mind gettin' that cocktail watch as I'm an early riser. Beans again, cookie?"

Micah Cade said flat-panned, "Lots of iron in 'em."

27

Around her now the talk flowed, with the campfire flaring down and Ira Hembree removing his kettles. Before long they'd seek their bedrolls and settle in for the night. But not for Reba Jo Cade, as she'd be going out to take her turn at watching the herd, by her father's big, turnip-shaped watch in about twenty minutes. Standing watch with her would be Felix Armijo. And to-night she was itching to get out there, tired as she was. For of late Reba Jo had found it hard fall-ing asleep. She was getting itchy-footed to get to Billings, to turn around right away and head for Texas and the waiting arms of Guy Jarrett.

Abruptly she rose and in passing told Armijo in a quiet undertone she was going to saddle one of her horses. The Mexican seemed to sense Reba Jo's mood, as he jackknifed to his feet and strode over to put his eating utensils in the washpan perched on the tailgate of the chuck wagon. He followed after Reba Jo, his eyes going of their own volition to take in the dark landscape and any clouds moving in. More than anything she made him think about Guy Jarrett, and of how Guy had given him a chance when he'd been just another drifter. "Sí, it is right that he marry Se-ñorita Cade."

The first hour of her watch went quickly for Reba Jo, saddlebound and alone except for when she came upon Armijo passing the opposite way as they circled the herd. Sometimes she'd catch bits of the Spanish songs sung by Armijo, and joined in. She couldn't stop worrying about Guy. Had he recovered from that operation? Did he miss her? Before hooking up with his brother to become a rancher, Guy Jarrett had been a Texas

Ranger, and still had in him a restless nature.

"And he's darned good-looking," Reba Jo flung out worriedly. "Could be some other Texas belle has got her hooks into him. Darn, wish this was over with and we were tracking back home."

Chapter Two

"Mako—isn't that some kind of shark?"

"My old man was a whaler."

His name really was Mako, Mako Brazelton. While the moniker had been hung on Mako Brazelton by the police out at San Francisco's infamous Barbary Coast, he'd headed a gang made up of his brothers and a bunch of waterfront scum. Muggings, white slavery, prostitution, shanghaiing the unwary aboard clipper ships, and other lowlife crimes had been Mako Brazelton's specialties. Causing his downfall was Brazelton's trying to muscle in on territory claimed by the Barbary Coast Chinese. Out of this came a bloodletting war. In order to keep the Chinatown Tongs out of it, the police raided Mako Brazelton's pierside saloon. Gavin and Joey Brazelton and other gang members were arrested, but somehow the elusive Mako eluded the police dragnet. Before cutting out he posted bond for his brothers, left word as to his new location.

Which proved out to be the copper camp of Butte, territorial Montana. He didn't arrive with a lot of ready cash. But he discovered promptly this mining camp striking onto the western slopes of the Rockies was tailor-made for a man with his considerable talents. The gaming action included horse racing and boxing matches, with racetrack poolrooms found in most of the camp's gambling resorts. Unlike the city on the bay, San Francisco, here Mako Brazelton found that the moneymen were on a first name basis with the miners. It was through a local character and racehorse tout named Colonel Buckets that he was introduced to some mine owners.

A charming rogue, as one West Coast judge had called him, Mako Brazelton had thick, curly black hair and a blue-black tint to his smoothly-shaven face. Always impeccable of manners and dress, he soon became part of an inner circle of those ruling the roost in Butte. What he learned he stowed away, as Brazelton decided early-on he wanted in on this mining game.

The winter of 1887 gave him that opportunity: the horrific storms wiping out entire herds of cattle. Borrowing what he could from his newfound friends, Mako Brazelton, now reunited with his brothers, sent cattle buyers down to Texas. As reports circulated up that a few ranchers would make the long drive to Butte, Mako and his brothers took a Northern Pacific train to Billings. Here the Brazeltons met secretly with an old-time Montana cow thief and gunhand, Brock Lacy. Once a deal had been struck, Gavin Brazelton stayed on in Billings to head this part of Mako's sinister operation.

It wasn't until the middle of summer that the first herd passed up the Bozeman trail. Once the herd cleared the Crow Indian Reservation, out

31

from Billings rode Gavin Brazelton and stock hands to take charge of the cattle, and with no protests from the Texans. Once the herd was hazing away, Gavin Brazelton told of a nearby hog ranch where they could close the deal. The promise of a hot bath and plenty of hard liquor, tied in with the money Brazelton was packing along, brought the trail-worn Texans northeasterly through humps of higher land scored with caves. There truly was a hog ranch a short distance away on the lane they followed, a known hangout for highliners. But then it happened, Brock Lacy and his men opening up with their long guns. Anticipating this, Gavin Brazelton had spurred his bronc away. If any survived, though few did, the outlaws closed in to finish the job. Next came the grisly part, the bodies being disposed off in one of the caves, but not before these hardcases had stripped the bodies of valuables. While this was going on, away went Gavin Brazelton back to Billings. There he supervised the loading of the cattle into boxcars bound for Butte.

Once the cattle arrived in Butte, Mako Brazelton had a lot of eager buyers. Though it went against his principles, he paid back the money he'd borrowed, salted the rest away in local banks. Overall four herds made the long trek up from Texas, and out of the last bunch through Mako Brazelton had culled out a big black bull, which he was studying at the moment from an upper smoking room in the main pavilion of Columbia Gardens.

The resort was located in a canyon about three miles east of Butte. The main pavilion had promenade verandas and balconies and a huge dance floor, while a stream cascading from higher up on the mountain supplied water for the flower gardens, fountains, and lawns cut through by pathways. On this late Saturday afternoon the crowd was mostly men, out here to see what Mako Brazelton's bull could do against a grizzly bear. The betting was typical of this mining camp, in the thousands, with free vittles being served in the banquet room and all the whiskey or beer a man could guzzle down.

"When it comes to horse racing or cards, Mako, you're damned lucky."

"Luck," laughed Mako Brazelton, "yes, without that a man might's well pack it in." He touched his glass against that held by Orrin Cartier, owner of the Ruby Mine. "Luck to you today, Orrin."

"A bull, I don't know. Did you see the size of that grizz? Biggest bear I've ever seen."

"So, Mr. Cartier, how are you wagering?"

"I hate to buck you, Mako, but . . . reckon it's on the bear."

"Just place your wagers over there." There was a tug at Mako Brazelton's sleeve. He sidled a glance that way. The frown was for his brother's companion, obviously a girl of the line. And that Joey Brazelton had been drinking was quickly noticeable. He'd learned to keep his brother close at hand, not that he didn't trust Joey, but the youngest of the Brazeltons often let his craving to have a good time hold sway over everything else. Sweeping a glance about the crowded room, Mako leaned in and whispered,

"About time you settled down."

"Aww, Mako, its goin' onto Saturday night."

33

Grittily he said, "Just don't botch things. The judge?"

"Why I came up. He just showed."

Nodding, Mako Brazelton had a smile for the ruby-lipped woman gussied up in a flaming red dress. His eyes flicking back to his brother, he pulled out his wallet, "Here, a couple of hundred; that should tide you over the weekend. But remember, Joey, keep family matters to yourself."

"Thanks, Mako," said Joey Hazelton, not as tall at around five-nine, more swarthy of face, adorned with a trim mustache and he had unruly black hair coming onto his shoulders. Back on the Barbary Coast he'd pimped for a string of street girls, and also did odd-job chores for Mako. Unbeknownst to Joey Brazelton was of his contacting syphilis, which would eventually cause his demise, and was, in fact, already producing moments of confusion. He sported a hideout gun tucked in a shoulder holster under the folds of the flannel suit coat, a cocky grin for his whore-of-the-moment as they hurried toward the staircase.

The other Brazelton in the room had also brought a young woman out to enjoy the afternoon's festivities. Daphnie Coleman returned Mako's smile as he threaded around a table. She held out a gloved hand, which he grasped but remained standing, nodding at others seated there. "Mako, wasn't that your brother?"

"Joey, yup. Just wanted to place a bet." He turned to a passing waiter holding a trayful of wineglasses, picked up one and set it down before Daphnie Coleman, a vivacious woman with dark red hair and possessed of considerable wealth, in

34

that her father owned the Dakota Mine. Divorced a second time a scant month ago, she was still in her early twenties. She had on a choker with black gemstones and matching pendant earrings, the low-cut black sequined dress showed a lot of creamy flesh, and there was her reckless laughter. That she was overly fond of Mako Brazelton could be detected in those glances she kept throwing at him. And a flicker of resentment as he kept up a running conversation with the men at the table.

"Mako honey, I'd like another drink."

"Sure," he said easily.

"Hey," someone called out. "Fifteen more minutes until post time."

"Post time—this isn't no hoss race, Arty. Yup, folks, you can watch from up here or down close to the action."

There came a scraping of chairs as most of those in the smoking room sought the staircase. A few lingered to place final wagers, which were covered by Mako Brazelton's men scattered throughout the pavilion. Moving with Daphnie Coleman to an open window, he struck flame to a wooden match, and held it to a cigarillo. Below, across a pathway, was an arena of reinforced planking encircled by a low, open grandstand of plank seats. Going onto dusk, workmen were propping ladders against light post to climb up and put flame to large lanterns.

"Whatever gave you the idea to do this?"

"The need, Miss Coleman, to acquire more cash."

"You're that sure your bull will win?"

"Hell, Daphnie, just what is a sure thing?

35

Maybe rigging a horse race or a deck of cards. Nope, I swear—" he held up protesting hands. "I didn't slip that grizzly a Mickey Finn. By the way, I hear your father, to put it bluntly, hates my innards."

"Told you before, Mako," she said while slipping an arm around his waist, "I don't give a damn what my pappy cares about."

"Aren't you afraid he'll cut you out?"

She tiptoed up to nip at his earlobe, and to whisper huskily, "Just beginning to realize the men I was married to before were barely out of puberty."

"You sure you went to a finishing school back east?"

"Hated every damn minute of it, Mako honey. Getting back to my father. I'm the only kin he has. He hated to see me get married the first time . . . the second time."

"I suppose your mother passing away has something to do with it."

"Yup, Mako, in spades. So, what about us?"

"I told you I loved you." He touched his lips to her cheek, then he brought his eyes sweeping to the arena as a silvertip grizzly appeared. From the opposite end of the arena came the raged bellowing of a bull as it caught the scent of the bear, now standing up and pawing at the darkening air. The din of the spectators fell away for a moment as did some of them pressing in close to the high wall of planking.

A gate sprang open and out of a holding pen charged the bull, a massive hulk of black flesh stretched over two thousand pounds of muscle and

36

sinew, springing forward with lowered head. The grizzly dropped down and stumbled away from that first charge, swiping out at the bull with a clawed foreleg. Foam spilled out of its nostrils, and the bull came in again as the silvertip rose up to stand its ground. Though the bull's right horn scored a hit, a giant claw slashed out and tore a large hunk from its shoulder. Now the grizzly flung itself over the bull's shoulders, and at the same time gouged dripping red flesh from the bull's flanks and rump.

In the horror of what was happening the crowd of about a thousand had fallen silent. Out of the bull came a frenzied roaring as the bull managed to break loose, although it was gory with blood from deep claw slashes. But it came in again to hook and butt at the bear, its blood staining the sand floor of the arena as it kept gushing out. The silvertip seemed to be having the better of it, and then it happened, the underpinnings of the grizzly slipped in a pool of blood. Instantly the bull rushed in, hooking and goring and stamping with its hooves until the grizzly, down now and pawing helplessly, was just a pile of lacerated flesh and broken bones.

"Oh, Mako," shuddered Daphnie Coleman "how horrible."

"Seen worse," he muttered, as the bull dropped to its knees and suddenly rolled over, dying but victorious. "Look, I've got some business to tend to. We can get together later tonight." He returned her nod, and then strode across the varnished hardwood floor and hurried down the staircase.

Crossing the dance floor, it was Mako Brazelton

37

sorting out the deal he would tender to Judge Homer Rayburn. A bewhiskered, curbstone lawyer, Rayburn came to Butte from a backward district in Missouri. That Homer Rayburn had been elected to a judgeship at all had come as a surprise since he seemed to spend more time in the cheaper saloons than at his office. But as Brazelton had found out, and others, to their sorrow, Rayburn, being a shrewd Southern trader with a glib tongue, got his name listed on the fall election ballots. Buttonholing delegates at the Democratic convention, he asked them to vote for him on the first ballot, "Not that he expected to be nominated, but for the advertising value." To the surprise of all but Homer Rayburn, the results of the first ballot showed he had a majority of the votes.

"This the room?"

"Rayburn's waiting inside, Mr. Brazelton."

"Keep a lookout," Mako Brazelton ordered as he twisted the doorknob to shoulder into a small room reeking of cigar smoke. Between Mako and the judge gazing out a window was an oaken table speckled with cigar ashes. The whiskey bottle on the table rested in a pool of spillage and he grimaced. The judge swung around on unsteady legs and yanked the cigar stub out of his mouth.

"Got a damned headache, Mako. Why don't we table this until later . . ."

"You've had plenty of time to hash it over, Judge."

"Maybe I have at that," he grumbled, and then he sat down heavily, a big man getting bigger and clad in an untidy black suit bearing old stains. The string tie hung over the inner vest, while gray-

38

ish smudges showed along the collar of the faded white shirt. He wore no hat, but in his blued-out eyes there was a speculating glimmer. "Bribery's against the law, Mako."

"A business partnership isn't," snapped Brazelton, as he sat down.

"Humph, that's a hoss of a different color— bonded green, which chances to be my favorite. A smelter, you said?"

A first meeting between them, about a month ago, had consisted of Mako Brazelton telling of his desire to build a smelter and, as he'd explained, for the alleged purpose of reducing the copper ore of the independent Butte mining operators who had no smelting facilities of their own. With the smelter about completed, the next step for Mako was to purchase his own mine in order, he'd explained, to assure keeping his smelter running to full capacity.

"You're a clever one, Mako. It took me some to figure that out. The smelter, bah." Judge Homer Rayburn tempered his retort with a yellow-toothed smile. "Holes, Mako, you'll be digging holes in the ground . . . scattered about, I'm sure . . . but always close to the bigger mines such as the Anaconda or Clark properties."

"That's where you come in, Homer."

"Indeed I do. As once they catch on, they'll be hauling your ass off to court." He reached a veined hand for the whiskey bottle, enjoying the byplay of words, and the chance to cut a deal. "Legal proceedings can be damned costly."

"Just make sure that my appearances are before your bench, Homer."

"There's more." Shrewd eyes rolled around in Judge Rayburn's black-browed sockets.

"Politics is the name of the game here," agreed Mako. "To beat the big money boys I've got to control the city and county governments. Otherwise laws can be passed to hinder my plans. I take it you're in, Homer . . ."

"Have been ever since our first chat. That bull out there, wasn't it railroaded in from Big Timber way?"

"You know it was."

"If I was you, Mako, I'd get out of the cattle business. Been far too many unexplained killings in that direction."

His eyes filming over, Mako Brazelton realized that the judge was as shrewd as they come. But could Judge Homer Rayburn be a danger to his plans? No, as all Rayburn really wanted was that judgeship and the strutting trappings that came with it, and a helluva lot of money.

"One more herd is coming through, so I've been told. Then I'm out of the cattle business. And it won't be too much longer before I'll own my first mine."

"That filly you brought along have anything to do with it?"

Laughing as he reached into an inner coat pocket, Mako Brazelton said, "Her old man does own a mine. Soon it'll be mine . . . and a lot of others." His hand dipped out holding an envelope, open and thick with greenbacks. Here, and just remember, Homer, bonded green is my favorite color, too."

40

Chapter Three

The last of the herd and a few laggards came up the mud-churned bank after the main body of cattle. Spreading out now in mid-afternoon, sunlight dappling their drying hides and the Texans breathed sighs of relief because the last ribbon of water had been crossed. None were more pleased than Micah Cade setting his horse into a lope after the two wagons. In passing Haw Butterfield, he flicked out his coiled lasso and drawled,

"Just one more day of this."

Butterfield called out, "About time as I'm worn to a frazzle."

Pulling alongside Ira Hembree sawing at his reins, Micah Cade said, "What do you think, Ira, we quit earlier today?"

"Okay with me if'n it sets right with Way. Thought someone was supposed to meet us by that creek."

"Today, tomorrow, all one and the same. Break out them peaches for supper, as there's no sense holding back on supplies now."

"Beans, won't hold back on 'em either, Micah."

41

"You ever eat a meal without 'em, Ira?"

"Recollect I do. But just remember this, nobody came down sickly on this here cattle drive. It was the iron in them beans done it."

"Lordy" Micah Cade jerked at his reins to wheel his bronc around—"when we hit Billings I'm gonna feast on mountain trout until I grow fins."

Throwing a glance at her father over where Ira Hembree was swinging his chuck wagon toward a treeline, Reba Jo Cade took in the lay of the hills westerly. They looked peaceful enough dusted as those low humps were with pines and grass fringing onto streaks of limestone, but despite this something didn't set well in her mind. A fretful worry squinting her eyes, Reba Jo reined after a steer holding back, while a short distance away, drag rider Buddy Keane took out after another laggard.

"Get," she yelled while slapping the steer across the rump with her coiled lasso. The steer bolted after the main herd strung out for 'bout three-quarters of a mile, and throwing back dust, she brought her bronc to a walk.

Anxiety brought on by the dream of last night brought her gazing distantly. Ever since sunup and through the day Reba Jo couldn't shake the feeling that something was out there amongst those hills. A few more miles and they'd clear the reservation—could be some Crow out there. She became aware of Buddy Keane straightening up in the saddle to take a gander northward. And Reba Jo did the same, spotting a few riders coming in through that gap passing between the creek bottom and the hills. He rode over, said dryly, "That's the cattle buyer, I reckon."

She barely heard him, as Reba Jo Cade looked beyond the spread of the herd, one gloved hand coming up to swipe a bottle fly from her furrowed brow. Taking in the worried set to her mouth, the ranny followed her gaze, and then Buddy Keane shrugged his tapering shoulders.

"Nothin' out there but more hills. But . . . you see something . . ."

"Guess it was just a dream after all," replied Reba Jo. Away from the right flank of the herd broke Shad Jarrett on his grulla, a reckless younker when the long drive started.

"End of the trail," he shouted upon coming back to them. "Cookie's gonna make camp just over that rise. And those from Billings are coming in."

"Tell us something we don't know," Keane said chidingly.

A quick smile danced in Reba Jo's eyes. "Don't pay him no mind, Shad. End of trail; never thought it would happen."

"You thinkin' of my uncle again?"

With a playful reach of her hand she slapped Shad Jarrett's hat away. "You damned right I am," came her salty retort.

The drovers spread out behind the man on the paint horse known only as Deal Falcone, a buyer for the Divide Cattle Company. That they didn't like Falcone was evident in the way they hung back, sneaking out spurious remarks about the flamboyant clothing worn by the man they

43

worked for, and that only a damnfool renegade Injun would ride a dappled paint.

As for the man riding the paint, he'd endured with a stoic patience the overheard barbs and the growing demands of outlaw chieftain Brock Lacy about getting a bigger share of the cut. Barrel-chested, and with his long legs dangling below the belly of his horse, Gavin Brazelton viewed what lay before him on the flat land east of the hills, the herd being bedded down and those working the cattle. Still about a quarter of a mile out, he doffed his big pearly-gray hat and waved it aloft. One of the drovers mimicked Brazelton's fawning smile spreading out under his handlebar mustache.

"Howdy, the camp."

Only one man rode out to greet the Billings delegation, Wayland Jarrett on his cutting horse, who slowed out of a lope to grasp Gavin Brazelton's outthrust hand. "Been a long time a-getting here."

"Jarrett, wasn't it?"

"Call me Way, Mr. Falcone." Twisting in the saddle, he took in the herd. "A lot of money tied up in them cows."

"Expect there is . . . and a lot of hopes and dreams, too, Way. Brought my drovers along."

Wayland Jarrett let his eyes sidle to the men slouched in their saddles, figured three were bonafide cowhands, the other seven men were more used to doing other work. He looked back at the cattle buyer. "How close are we to that trail's end town?"

"To Billings, sundown tomorrow should see us

44

getting in. But northeast of here, not all that far, is a place where a man can chase the elephant."

There was a spark of interest in Jarrett's pondering eyes.

"One of them hog ranches . . . but got a nice spread of buildings. A place where a man can sleep under a roof after soakin' trail-dust away in a hot tub. I'll pick up the tab, Way, as that's the least I can do."

"Mighty generous," he smiled back. "Well, we'll tend to the cattle first . . ." He left it there, then reining around, Wayland Jarrett began jogging his horse back.

By the time the haze of blue shadows were spreading out to darken the hills, the Texans had pulled away from the cattle that had settled in for the night. A brightening of the lower sky eastward gave promise of another full moon. This, and the fact they were finally here, should have served to lighten up Reba Jo's thoughts. The drovers were what they appeared to be, and she'd let it go at that. A different matter was the cattle buyer. There was an aura of arrogance, something else that she couldn't quite nail down. Dreams; there'd been a lot of them lately. Mostly about Guy Jarrett and of things that had happened along the trail.

When Gavin Brazelton, Micah, and Way Jarrett moved in to palaver closer to the campfire, she let her eyes play intently over the cattle buyer's swarthy face. He had a chip-toothed smile and reckless eyes shaded by that low brim. He had a cocky, devil-may-care laugh, which those around her responded to, and in her was a moment of

45

resentment. *A damned gladhander,* was Reba Jo's musing. There was something in the dark green eyes, or was it just the rising flames of the campfire pitching out distorting waves.

"Settled, then," exclaimed Micah Cade.

"Yup, appears like it," ventured Wayland Jarrett. "You sure your men can handle the remuda and fetch our wagons along?"

From where he stood by the chuck wagon, Ira Hembree said, "Won't mind turning my wagon over . . . none a'tall."

"You'll be leavin' all them sacks of beans behind, Ira."

"Dang you, Haw Butterfield, they was manna from heaven way I fixed 'em."

Laughter resounded around the campfire. And soon they were heading for their horses, leaving bedrolls and possible sacks behind, to catch up with all of this and the herd sometime tomorrow. Once they were back across the creek, the cattle buyer brought them northeasterly.

"You didn't say too much back there."

"I'm worried, Pa."

Micah Cade rubbed at his chin; a thoughtful gesture. He said quietly, "About getting back to Guy?"

"That . . . and . . . guess its just the way I feel . . ."

"Feelings go a long way—an' sometimes to lead you astray, Reba Jo."

"What do you make of Mr. Falcone?"

"Kind of a braggard; the usual run of cattle buyer. Even I've got to admit he's some fancy dresser. That blue suit sort of matches up with

46

that paint hoss he's astride. But, Reba Jo, as long's he's got our money . . ."

In passing through a narrows and away from the sullen waters of Pryor Creek, Reba Jo felt a sudden chill which caused her to yank back on the reins: her bronc sidestepped in protest. A soft word brought her horse back in line on a vague track set to drumming and flinging out a few pebbles from underneath their mounts. Emerging from the narrows, they rode into spreading moonlight. Up front rode Wayland Jarrett, and next to him the cattle buyer, Falcone, the words of Falcone hearty and coming back along the walking horses.

"Damned," Reba Jo muttered silently between clenched teeth, "I wish that damned bigmouth would hush up."

Kyle Foley, riding just in front of her, gestured to rising heights a short distance away which were dotted with cave openings, the tops of these heights rock-shaly and flat. The lane widened into a meadow carpeted with the dying grass of summer, but still greened out some. Here everyone spread out to give themselves elbow room, and grins appeared when the cattle buyer flung out it wasn't more'n a mile to that hog ranch.

"A little whiskey'll uncake the dust from my throat."

"Maybeso, Butterfield, but it'll take a heap more lye soap to clean all of this grime away. They got clean sheets at this hog ranch?"

"Listen to Foley — clean sheets. Next he'll be wantin' room service."

To Wayland Jarrett's surprise the cattle buyer

suddenly spurred his paint horse into a fast canter, while the Texan remained undecided as to the ways of it or to do the same. Still puzzling over this, Jarrett glanced about, the rocky heights above which the moon was camping over, and opposite. In the drawn-back darkness of this moonlit night he couldn't make out any movement, just the sounds of those he rode with coming back to him. Then it came and all at once, the throaty varooming of rifles.

Back amongst the others, Reba Jo Cade heard the whacking of a leaden slug followed by Buddy Keane's cry of pain. As she tried to control her frightened bronc, men and horses were going down around her. Muzzle flashes came from both sides of the small meadow, but the only thing Reba Jo was aware of was that her horse staggered and spilled her out of the saddle. She went over backward and hit hard, the shod hoofs of her dying horse striking inches from her prone body.

Micah Cade, looking about wild-eyed for his daughter, sustained another hit to his midriff that drove the wind out of him. Then he was falling out of the saddle, dying, but still trying to shout, "Reba . . . Reba . . . Jo . . ."

Wayland Jarrett had been one of the first to be hit, but somehow he held to the saddle, a man confused but still managing to claw out his sidearm. Only there wasn't anything to shoot at, and then he remembered the cattle buyer pulling freight, and somehow he reined his horse that way. He got as far as some thorny bushes hedging in on the meadow when one of the ambushers

48

let go a slug that tore into his lower back, the horse under Jarrett started to pitch and buck and rag doll him away. He didn't remember falling into the thorns of a large bush as everything went black.

Just like that the firing stopped, with the awful reverberating of all that gunfire still screaming at the two men still asaddle out in the meadow, one of them being Shad Jarrett, and a few paces away, a hatless Ira Hembree. There was a sharp whistle, then vague shadows came cautiously into view. Shad Jarrett, shocked by the viciousness of it all, tried holding back the tears, then he shuddered and began crying. "Pa . . . Pa . . . help me . . ."

"One of them's a kid."

Spearing up his hands, Ira Hembree twisted his head and hissed, "Shad, hang in there, boy, I . . ."

Varoom! The man cutting loose with his Colt's was outlaw Brock Lacy, the bullet slamming into Ira Hembree's heart killing him instantly. The body fell limply out of the saddle. Lacy triggered his six-gun again as an afterthought, and spread his lips in a pleased grin when he did.

"What about the kid?"

"I want him."

Brock Lacy looked at the hard case who'd said that, and shook his head ruefully. "You know the way of it, Thatch, no survivors."

Coming in on the fringe of the meadow was Gavin Brazelton, and he said brittlely, "He dies, now." To put weight to his words Brazelton unleathered his handgun. Then he wheeled his horse about and tried to hit a shadowy figure pushing thorny brush aside. "Get him!"

While some of his men took out after Wayland Jarrett trying to get away, Brock Lacy held there as the cattle buyer rode closer. His eyes flicked to the hard case named Thatch grabbing the down-hitched reins and working his way back along the horse to Shad Jarrett humped over crying in the saddle. Then Lacy looked up at the man he'd hired and said in icy undertones,

"Look, Falcone, you killin' sonofabitch, Thatch over there hasn't had a boy in a long time. After he's had his pleasure Thatch don't do the job I'll pump a round into the kid. Anyways, Thatch is fast, faster'n either of us. So what's it to be . . . ?"

"Later, then."

They moved in to the downed mass of horses and Texans looking to finish their killing task, and it was about here that a hard case stumbled over Reba Jo fighting to open her eyes.

"Dammit, a woman, a woman!"

"Dead?"

The outlaw dropped to his knees and pawed over her body for any signs of blood. "Appears not to be hit; hoss must have thrown her."

"Get her up so's all of us can take a gander," ordered Brock Lacy, careful to keep an eye on the cattle buyer still gripping that sidearm of his. "Say, now, she's a helluva looker."

"Too bad."

"You gonna kill a woman?"

Gavin Brazelton through compressed lips said, "The deal was everyone must die."

50

At that moment Reba Jo Cade, conscious now and aware of being held up, screamed at the awful enormity of what the cattle buyer had just uttered, fully aware that around her all of the others were dead. One of the hard cases thrust in a hand and tore away the front of her woolen shirt to expose the abalone pearl necklace. At the sight of it Gavin Brazelton stepped closer and broke it away from her neck. He said,

"She's a comely bitch awright, Lacy. Will give some pleasure to your men."

"Me to, I expect. Hog-tie her and load her aboard a spare hoss. But for now we've got to clean up this mess. So, Falcone, I expect I'll see you back at Billings."

"I'll be there. There won't be any more herds coming up from Texas."

"Expected this to end sometime. Billings."

Thrusting the necklace into a coat pocket, Gavin Brazelton reclaimed his saddle and the southeasterly trail that would fetch him back to the trail herd. There came to him the rattling of gunfire, to let it settle in his mind that Lacy's men had caught that straggler. But Brazelton would have headed back had he known that Wayland Jarrett had made it up into the rocks and stood a chance of getting away.

Under the brassy glare of moonlight Wayland Jarrett dragged his wounded body deeper into a recession slanting up the hillside. His clothing ribboned by thorny brush were dampened with sweat and blood. His holster was empty, his mind

51

unable to fully comprehend all of this. Below and around him he could hear the ambushers, once in a while a gun sounded to have sparks screech away from rock.

"My fault . . . should have caught on . . . but . . ." Desperation brought him ignoring the pain of his wounds, brought him crawling on, as he'd been doing for the past few hours.

Like a prairie dog checking things beyond its den, Way Jarrett rose up on weakening legs as the moon sought the cover of a cloud. Somehow he pressed upward, a survivor's instinct behind that move, and was vaguely aware that first light couldn't be far off. As he did so, some of the ambushers began turning back.

"I know I hit him."

"Yeah, won't last long."

"Me, I'm keeping after that ranny," said a rail-thin hard case named Alcorn, and the others left him there, that pork sticker knife of Alcorn's clutched in one hand and the Henry in the other. What he hadn't told the others was that he came across blotches of fresh blood just downslope on a boulder. What he wanted was the spoils, and to use his knife. Agilely, he crab-legged over a few blocking rocks and grabbed for support the trunk of a limber pine, pressing upward.

"I told you so," Alcorn exulted upon working his way over rimrock to find the inert form of the Texan in a stand of pines, just the hint of a morning breeze rustling the branches. He leaned the rifle against a low pine branch and discovered the wounded man was still alive. "Damned unlucky for you, Texas."

He turned the body over and kicked Wayland Jarrett into awareness. The moon had vacated and the sky lightened into daylight. He grinned wickedly at the Texan trying to focus in on him. "You ain't in Hades yet . . . but you'll wish you were before long."

Wayland Jarrett tried pushing up to get at the hard case, who just laughed. "You're so weak you can't even reach around to scratch at your butt, Texas." Then Alcorn dropped down to grab a hunk of Jarrett's hair, held it firmly as he brought the blade of his needle-sharp hunting knife slicing into the eye socket.

The shock of what was happening ripped a frenzied scream out of Wayland Jarrett, with his hands, he groped for a loose rock. Somehow his left hand closed around one. Somehow he summoned enough strength to hit the ambusher in the head, and Alcorn spilled sideways. Like a trapped mountain lion, Jarrett grappled for the knife. He didn't know he'd gained possession of it or that he had plunged it into the ambusher's chest until the man went limp. All Wayland Jarrett knew was the new and agonizing pain coming from his empty eye socket. Then, in the dawning of a new day, he lost consciousness.

The brother of Guy Jarrett was still alive a day later, barely, but with enough strength to literally crawl off that hill. And then he wished he hadn't, since he came upon tracks passing out of the meadow and to a low cave mouth. What spilled out of it was the stench of death, but Wayland Jarrett had to know, and he crawled on into the cave.

And he wished he hadn't because more screams tore out of Wayland Jarrett as he viewed the mangled bodies of his fellow Texans, as something snapped in his mind. Later that day a Crow hunting party stumbled upon what remained of Wayland Jarrett.

Chapter Four

There were still the railroad tracks to cross on the eastern flanks of Billings. But Guy Jarrett held up the claybank on a patch of prairieland. West of this rimrock town, according to the maps he'd studied, it was one jagged mountain range after another. Along his backtrail lay the Crow Indian Reservation. Although he'd picked up old sign of cattle passing through the reservation, no white men lived there to tell him the harsh truth of what had happened.

Right at the moment he felt as lonely as any cowhand had a right to be, and gaunted a lot from long days of holding to the saddle. And too, sometimes food didn't settle right in his belly, and Guy would shove up to leave. Another matter of concern to the rancher from Texas was his dwindling cash supply. About broke, he opined.

Chips was the name he'd coined for the claybank, not for any particular reason, or maybe it was because the hoss was kind of chippy first thing in the mornings. But it was a stayer, with a rocking chair gait.

"Hate to sell you," Guy said idly, more to hear

his voice than anything else. Farther westward he took in the main shipping pens strung along the right-of-way. While the main clutch of buildings lay north of the tracks, a lot of them showing new timber. "At least up here they're making money."

Moving on, the claybank snorted nervously when the steel rails they were crossing began humming to announce a train chugging in from the east. Riding parallel to the tracks, Guy Jarrett studied the cattle stirring about in the holding pens. The brands they carried were unknown to him, but the herd he was seeking had been brought here. That was about the only thing he was sure of, and that being a cattle town, there would be the usual run of livestock companies. Farther along he came upon cattle being driven up a ramp into a boxcar.

"Hiyyeee, get up there . . ."

"Look out for them horns."

Standing up on the side railing was a cowhand wearing jaded out clothes and a stubble of beard on a long face bored by all of this, the long switch he held striking out to keep the cattle heading into the boxcar. He became aware of the watching horseman, took a casual glance, threw a nod at Guy.

"You don't want to work here."

"Nope, reckon not. These cattle being shipped to Butte?"

"Expect they are, mister."

"These cattle come up from the south . . . ?"

"Nah, local stuff . . . and kind of scrawny, too. But them miners over in Butte'll tackle anything."

"Hey you, Lafferty," yelled a man hurrying

down a runway passing between holding pens, "get back to watching them cattle."

"The yard boss," muttered the cowhand to Guy Jarrett, and Guy said, "Maybe I'll see you around town." He brought the claybank around and away from the holding pens.

He left behind Eddy Lafferty puzzling over the J-J brand on the stranger's bronc. A longtime cowhand, Lafferty could recall a lot of brands he'd run across. Older now, and not so anxious to go back to the daily grind of being a full-time waddy, he'd hired on as a stock handler to be closer to the comforts of Billings.

"What did he want?"

"Directions to a good hotel," responded Lafferty just as rudely. Savagely he flicked out at the last of the cattle reluctant to enter the boxcar. "Someone put salt in your coffce . . . ?" But when he turned to look, the yard manager, a former rancher named Tysdale, was moving away. A year ago it had been a pleasure working for Tysdale, but no more. That cattle buyer had a lot to do with it, and thinking on it now, Eddy Lafferty got to remembering that rep for the Divide Cattle Company had left shortly after the last herd up from Texas had come through. Falcone, yup, a glad-handing dandy. Stepping down into the mud of the runway, the brand those cattle had been sprouting took form in his mind's-cye—the J-J brand.

"Same as was decorating that hombre's hoss?"

Come to think on it, came Lafferty's musings, as he eyed the late afternoon sun, we brought that herd on in here. But none of those Texans ever showed up in town? There were other trail herds, too? Bypassing the main office where the other stock handlers were congregating, Lafferty eased onto a muddy street knifing into town.

That Texan . . . be interesting havin' a chat with him . . ."

No less an authority than the mayor of Billings told Guy Jarrett he hadn't heard of the Divide Cattle Company. The county sheriff not only affirmed this, but that few Texans had come in last summer. The sheriff, kind of roly-poly with a sagging walrus mustache, let the spoon he'd stirred his coffee with clatter onto his desk. "A farfetched story, Mr. Jarrett. Last letter you got was mailed out of Sheridan? But then, there's your brother down at that Indian mission." He drummed pondering fingers on his cluttered desk top, half believing the grisly tale told him by the Texan.

"The way I figure it, Sheriff . . ."

He held up a restraining hand. "Speculation doesn't help us much at this point in time. Ever since they started mining copper over at Butte a lot of folks have flowed through, mostly foreigners, but a heap of Westerners, too. If that herd of yours did arrive, a starting point would have to be those holding pens, which means sounding out Herman Tysdale."

"A big, chunky man?"

"That's Tysdale."

"The other cattle companies headquartering here also bought Texas beef; but from those hazing them up here."

58

"There are a few honest folks abouts, Mr. Jarrett."

Guy shoved up from the chair. In him was a well of emptiness, a weariness brought about by old wounds being scabbed and broke open. Yesterday had seen him break his last double eagle to pay for boarding his horse at a livery stable, and a dingy room in a dingier hostel. His eyes bittered into flint, he held the sheriff's gaze.

"Someplace out there are the graves of my friends, if they were buried at all. Murdered by . . ."

"I've got to believe you, Mr. Jarrett."

"Too bad cattle can't talk. But that herd has been sold and turned into hash by now."

"Butte, that's what this cattle buyer told you down in Texas. A lot of cattle were shipped there. A lot of con artists and the like pushed in there, too."

"Sheriff, think I'll stick around here, as Billings would be the final stopping place for trail herds. I'll be in touch."

Out under a shading porch visoring a hardware store crouched at a busy intersection of downtown Billings, Guy took out the Durham and wheat straw papers. Quoting the sheriff, it was a far-fetched story of an entire crew being taken out. But about Sheriff Mason Taylor was a look of dependability, which meant he'd probably send one of his deputies down to that Indian mission. Meanwhile, for Guy Jarrett, a gut feeling was building.

"There are people hereabouts who were mixed up in this. Just like down in Texas when I was

59

rangering, you just keep turning over rocks . . ."

The supper partaken of by Guy was a mess of lukewarm gravy over mashed potatoes and stringy beef, a meal he had to wash down with several cups of thick chicory coffee, as he was used to down in Texas. A few who'd eaten straggled out to leave Guy the only customer in a beanery with ugly yellow paint stuck to the walls and a lot of old calendars. The floor tiles were a worn patchwork of squares over hardwood and there was some litter. Behind Guy the screen door creaked open and he half-turned in the booth to look. The disinterested set to his eyes faded away as toward him ambled stock handler Eddy Lafferty.

"You're a hard man to find."

"Lafferty, wasn't it?"

Nodding, he eased in across from Guy, and tipped his hat back to show a lot of graying hair. He twitched his nose with his thumb, used the same hand to bring the only waiter up from a stool. "That beef's got a lot of gristle in it."

"Settles in hard."

"Coffee, bacon and eggs over easy." He looked back at Guy around an easy smile. "Just call me Eddy."

"Guy Jarrett." He shoved his plate aside.

"You've got that look . . . of being a once-upon-a-time lawman . . ."

Absorbing this through passive eyes, Guy realized there was a lot more to Lafferty than worn clothing and work-worn hands, that this man had some kind of past. The voice, though raspy-rough, was that of someone with an education. Guy waited until the waiter had filled Lafferty's cup

60

and left a fresh pot of coffee behind, then he said,

"Was with the Texas Rangers."

"Had a brush with 'em once." Lafferty smiled as he picked up his cup. "But as I said, Mr. Jarrett, you're a hard man to track down. Or maybe I had you figured for hanging around fancier places."

"Moncy only goes so far."

"Saw that J-J brand before."

Guy's shoulders touched back to brace against the high booth backing, his eyes blinking their surprise but holding to Eddy Lafferty, as Lafferty went on.

"One of the herds we went out to take over. Me and the other stock handlers, late last summer it was."

"A woman . . . you saw her . . . ?"

"Recollect I did. Awful pretty, too. Then they headed out with that cattle buyer, Deal Falcone."

"Headed out where?"

"Up northeasterly I guess, to a road ranch not all that far away. Left their wagons behind, and rigging and such, and bedrolls. Same thing happened when other herds came up. Jarrett, that's all I know. Those wagons? We drove them on in to Billings, where Tysdale took charge of them."

Guy Jarrett sat there filling in the gaps of what had happened. Across the narrow street a street lamp threw wavery light against the wide window-pane, and there was little movement on the street. This was as close, he mused, as he would come to the truth, as he was certain Lafferty had told the facts as he'd known them. Tysdale, the man in

61

charge of the stock pens, had the answers he wanted.

Window glass exploded inwardly showering the occupants of the booth with cutting fragments. But it wasn't shattered glass that sliced through Guy's hatband and grazed his upper forehead but a steel-jacketed slug. His hat fluttered away; Guy spun out of the booth and dropped to the floor, stunned by this sudden violence, and with enough presence of mind to slap a hand to his holstered six-gun. He looked up at Lafferty sagged in the booth and eyes gaping open, a bullet impacting into his chest, and Guy fired blindly out the window. Then he realized his was the only gun sounding, and he lifted his finger from the trigger.

Crouching up, he strode to the door and yanked the screen door open and went out to stand on the boardwalk. Off to his left and at a distance he heard the thudding of boots growing fainter. He held there, breathing heavily, a droplet of his own blood coming down to catch the corner of his eye. "Lafferty . . . guess he knew too much." Turning and releathering his sidearm, Guy went back inside.

Stooping to pick up his Stetson, he dropped some money on the countertop and said,

"Tell the sheriff I'll drop by his office."

"Sure, mister," stammered the waiter, "but just who in tarnation are you?"

"The sheriff'll know."

Striding outside and into the night streets of Billings, he found a passageway of a gravelly lane which led back the way he had come in, by those stock pens along the Northern Pacific right-of-way.

Twenty minutes later he was coming in on the pens, the cattle in them a blacker mass with here and there a white face showing or the tawniness of a Longhorn. To his surprise a light could be glimpsed in the office building. But it wasn't until Guy had worked around to the front of the building that he saw the horse and buggy.

"Tysdale, did he come back here after the shooting?" He held to the shadows pressing close around the building, as in his mind he chewed over what Lafferty had told him about the man owning that buggy. "Just doesn't seem to be the type . . . and, there was more'n one gun cutting away at us . . ."

Easing toward the open doorway, he slipped inside, the floorboards creaking under his boots, and he brought up his weapon. To his left a bullpen office, doors lining the wall opposite, light seeping out from under a closed door, and he went there, spun the knob and followed the opening door into the room.

Slumped over the only desk was the man he sought, blood staining the back of Tysdale's head, and the hand spread out over the desk top still clutching a pen. Guy stepped up to the desk and around to its side, and slowly he lifted Tysdale's hand away from the paper underneath.

A wavery and dying hand had scrawled—*Butte* . . . *Fal* . . .

Common sense, that cold clutch of reason, told him the killer could still be hanging around, and he stepped back so's not to be framed in the only window. Tysdale, as Eddy Lafferty detailed, had been running scared. Tysdale had contacted others involved in stealing those trail herds, which meant they were denizens of Billings. Had to be hired guns? Or money men, as some of them weren't too damned particular as to how they gained their wealth.

"Fal?" Guy puzzled over this as he vacated the room to leave the building. "There was mention by Lafferty of a Deal Falcone; got to be it. But . . . Butte?"

Deciding to take the buggy instead of making that long trek over to the sheriff's office, Guy untied the reins and went back to settle onto the front seat. He brought the buggy rattling across the tracks of a siding and northward, the throbbing of the wound a reminder that it had been pure luck his not getting killed. Another turn brought Guy onto one of the business streets still pouring out a lot of light as this was a gambling and drinking town.

"That's him!"

Just leaving the sheriff's office was the waiter from that beanery, with a deputy behind, and the sheriff there, too. Guy reined in toward the boardwalk. He climbed down stiffly.

"He tell you the truth of it, Sheriff?"

"Just like it happened . . . you and your friend chowing down . . . then all hell broke loose . . ."

"Seems you were hit, too, Jarrett."

"A flesh wound."

The sheriff took in the horse and buggy, and said quietly, "Seems I've seen that rig before . . ."

"The man owning it won't be using it again."

"Come on inside and tell me about it. Oh, Smithson, come by in the morning to sign a statement." To the jingling of his spurs the sheriff tramped back across the boardwalk and went into his office, as did Guy Jarrett. Untying the bandanna from around his neck, Guy doffed his hat as he stepped over to a wall table.

"Eddy Lafferty drifted in to where I was eating supper. Told me about him and others going out to meet those trail herds." He wet part of the bandanna in a water bucket, and began dabbing at the wound to wipe away the caked blood. He went on, "Tysdale was in on it."

"How do you figure that?"

"The message he managed to write before he died. Right after that ruckus over at that beanery, well, I took out for those shipping pens down by the NP tracks. I figure Tysdale was murdered before they came after us."

"A message . . ."

"Not much, really. There was one word, Butte, he managed to get out . . . and what I reckon to be the name of the person behind all of this."

"Care to share it with me?"

"Not much to share. Just three letters . . . F-A-L . . ."

"Got to be Deal Falcone. He hung around a lot last summer. Couldn't buy drinks fast enough, and some snapper dresser. Claimed to be a gambler, and maybe was."

"Seen him around town lately?"

"Nope, not since, not since last fall, come to think on it. So, Mr. Jarrett, seems I'm stuck with a pair of dead men. Reckon too, your story isn't so farfetched. I'll go take a look at that body. And you?"

"Probably head for Butte. Just a hunch I guess."

"By the way, I sent a telegram down to Texas. Seems you are a rancher after all. Had been a Texas Ranger, too. Nothing personal, Jarrett."

"You could talk to those other stock handlers."

"Had that in mind. Hope you find some answers over at Butte. I don't know, Jarrett, as I'd hold up under all you've been through."

"Man's got no other choice sometimes."

"This Reba Jo, well, good luck, Mr. Jarrett."

Only after he was ambling downstreet did Guy Jarrett dare say her name, let it hang in his thoughts for a moment before he steeled them to what lay ahead.

"Trail's end town isn't here but Butte. One thing for damned certain, it'll be the end of the trail for somebody."

"You had 'em dead to rights!"

Brock Lacy brought the quirt fastened to a thong encircling his wrist lashing out at a wall studding. Lacy's anger kept him pacing the bare wood floor in a back room of the Lazy Man Saloon. Muted laughter and honky-tonk music came down a back hallway to seep into the room, and when one of the hard cases reached for the pitcher of beer, it was Lacy slamming his quirt down on the tabletop.

"Damn, Brock," the hard case muttered as he drew his hand back, "these things happen."

"What happened is that you and Benson can't handle much of anything." The red shirt under

66

Lacy's plain leather vest deepened the angry blush distorting his face. Now the slanchwise stare took in the three men seated there. Hitching a boot on an empty chair, he tugged his holstered gun out of the way, then he slouched to drape an arm over his bent knee. "Pickings are damned slim around here."

"You got somethin' in mind, Brock?"

"With no more cattle coming up there's just the banks." Before, for Lacy and his men, along with the banks had been the stagecoaches to steal from. Now everyone rode the trains, which were a helluva lot harder to rob. Rustling had tapered off after that bad winter of 1887, and the range wasn't all that open anymore, what with a lot of homesteaders coming in on the trains. He took in his pack of killers, the remnants of what had once been a gang of ten.

"Tysdale had to be taken out."

"Why do we keep on doing that cattle buyer's dirty works Brock?"

"Just tidying up some loose ends," said Lacy. Less'n a week ago they'd left their hideout in the lofty Absarokas to make their way down to Red Lodge and a saloon they frequented. Passed on to Brock Lacy had been a telegram sent by Tydsdale, telling of that Texan coming in. This was something Lacy had talked over with that cattle buyer out of Butte, but instead of taking out Tysdale right away, Lacy's own telegram had been sent to Gavin Brazelton. The money he'd demanded in his wire was waiting when Brock Lacy and his men rode into Billings around noon that day. Their guns went into action later that night.

67

His eyes holding a faraway glimmer, Brock Lacy let his thoughts drift away to that night of violence along Pryor Creek. With the departure of Gavin Brazelton, Lacy and his hard cases had used their ropes to drag the dead bodies of those Texans into one of the caves just west of the meadow where the killings had taken place. While the bodies were being scavenged for money and other valuables, the dead horses were roped and taken into a gully and left for the carrion. Then the long ride back to their hideout had begun, with Thatch holding the reins of the bronc on which the boy rode, and there was the woman, too, which made the bunch of them all that more anxious to keep on the move.

The ghostly cavalcade passed through the settlement of Roscoe at cockcrowing time under a steely sky to follow the rising tangents of a draw. Around about them now loomed Mount Wood in the Absarokas. During the night whenever they'd pulled up to swig out their throats with water, or in some cases, whiskey, and to rest their horses, it would be Thatch tending to the boy hog-tied to his saddled horse, but the rest of them only had eyes for the woman. She spoke but once, and it was when Brock Lacy came up to offer her a drink from his canteen, and said with a leering smile,

"You'll give us a lot of pleasure."

"You murdering bastard!"

His gloved hand snaked out to backhand Reba Jo Cade across the cheek so hard that her head snapped back as he snarled, "I'm gonna take you first, bitch. Then watch while my men have their way . . ." And in the same sentence he yelled, "Dammit, mount up."

Reclaiming their horses, the outlaws brought them upward at a slow walk, in single file, off to their right the swelling and murmurous sound of falling waters. They were deeper in the mountain, its walls sheer around them and humping a lot higher. And around them, too, was the pine forest of the mountain, with nary a branch stirring in the cold of first light.

Numbly Reba Jo took all of this in, once in a while being able to sneak a glance back at Shad Jarrett humped low in his saddle. She was ever-conscious of her torn shirtfront, of goose bumps spreading across the creamy swell of her exposed flesh, and of how cold it was. Once one of them had stolen in when they'd stopped for a breather to reach past her bound arms and cup a hand inside her shirt to fondle her breast. Her curses had sent him laughing away.

To Reba Jo it seemed a part of her had been ripped away when that bogus cattle buyer had broken the necklace away from her neck. While the shock of it all, of these brutal killings, was so much a horrible nightmare. These men were heartless and mindless monsters, especially the one they called Thatch. If she could be grateful for anything, it was that Shad Jarrett didn't know what was in store for him.

The outlaw holding the reins of her horse jerked on them to flick Reba Jo's eyes to him, and to have the outlaw nod rightward at the jagged trail they would have to take, the high rocks breaking away beyond the cascading falls misting out water and roaring eerily.

Brock Lacy's voice came in a muted shout, "Watch yourself now, dammit, as there's been some rockfall lately."

"I'll watch the hussy," a hard case shouted back.

The column of riders held up to pass along the narrowing of the trail in single file, and warily. It came to Reba Jo then, forgetting the pain of the ropes chafing and lacerating her wrists, that she could not let these mad dogs destroy her body. She owed this to the man she loved. As for the boy, he must fend for himself. Choking down her fear and blanking out all of her thoughts, Reba Jo brought up her legs to jab both of her spurred boots into the belly of her bronc as she screamed out,

"Hiyyeee!"

The bronc bolted forward and tore the reins away from the hard case's gloved hand. One moment Reba Jo's horse touched onto gravelly track, the next both horse and rider catapulting away into the darkening maw of what lay below.

There was a moment of confusion among the outlaws, then one of them yanked out his six-gun and triggered away at the man just holding the reins of the woman's horse. Quickly other guns were pounding away as a sort of angry frenzy overtook the outlaw gang. A couple went down with Brock Lacy's gun out and taking a sneak shot at Shad Jarrett. He scored a solid hit as Thatch became aware of what was happening he shouted,

"No, he's mine!" The outlaw went for his six-gun, but never got it out as Brock Lacy fanned the hammer of his gun twice. As Thatch lurched out of the saddle to fall alongside the outer edge of the trail, Lacy shouted,

"Cease firing, dammit! It's over!"

With the acrid stench of gunpowder lifting away, and with more sunlight dappling upon the mountainside, the outlaws took stock of what had just happened. Lacy knew it was all because of the woman, but he couldn't vent his anger now, not up here where the slightest misstep would be a man's undoing. He swung his bronc over to take in the large pool of water at the bottom of the cataract and beyond the rapids spilling foaming water around boulders. Nobody, he mused, could survive that fall. As for his killing Thatch, it had been something that had been building. Thatch should have known better than to keep that boy alive, but he hadn't, and Brock Lacy figured he was just doing what the cattle buyer wanted.

The hard case Benson rode up. "Millard's dead . . . an' Johnson's hit damned bad, Brock."

"Too damned bad. Finish Johnson off, then we'll take his hoss and anything of value. Then pitch all of 'em over where that woman jumped." And before pulling away from the drop-off side of the track, Lacy squinted again through the thick misty water near the bottom of the gorging waterfall, then muttered, "To hell with it, she's a goner."

At first the undertow which had held Reba Jo Cade under the surface seemed determined not to let go of her. When it finally did, she surged gasping to the surface only to have the foaming rapids

71

carry her downstream, tumbling, still with her hands tied. She could scarcely believe she was still alive, and expected at any moment to have the undertow suck her under and dash her against the lurking rocks. Then she got hung up as the current swung her into a jumble of debris caught in boulders out in midstream. The rapids were a deafening roar, her mind reeled when, to her horror the dead horse she'd jumped over those high rocks spilled by, the saddle somehow still cinched to its back. That it wasn't flailing out with its legs told Reba Jo the horse was dead.

"Climb up," she told herself, but then the debris tore away from the recession in the rocks taking her back into the twisting rapids spilling into lower pockets of the down-running creek. Somehow she managed to hang on to a broken tree branch even when everything started going black around her. Numbed with the shock of the fall and the icy water, it took Reba Jo a while to figure out she was in calmer water forming a catch basin under an overhanging cliff. Soon she felt rocky bottom, pulled herself out and flopped down on rocks smoothened by water erosion. As she simply let unconsciousness take over, Reba Jo was unaware of the dead horse intruding into her watery haven.

Magpies chattering away brought awareness to Reba Jo, this, and something tapping away at one of her boots. At first her comprehension of where she was eluded her. Then she spun catlike onto her back, to find that somehow she'd pulled herself out of the watery basin, with the magpies fluttering away.

"Git, you damned scavengers," she said weakly.

For a while her eyes wouldn't focus, but she shook away the blackness trying to clutch at her mind, and then it all came back to her, that her hands were still tied together, and everything else.

It was about then she noticed the dead horse hugging in against the rocky bank. Farther away and downslope huge winged creatures dipped down to follow the murmurous creek. Vultures could only mean something or someone else had died, and she blurted out,

"Could it be Shad Jarrett?" Her face twisted into an agonizing mask, and the tears came for Reba Jo Cade.

"Damn them . . . damn those scummy killers . . ."

She clenched her hands together as sobs racked her body, and only then did Reba Jo realize there were abrasions on her arms and body caused by striking into boulders during that terrifying watery passage to this catch basin. With this knowledge came a surge of pain, that her upper garments had been about tattered away. Deep here in this canyon it was shadowy, and no longer could she see the sun, figured it was late afternoon. First she had to free her hands, and despite the pain as she struggled to her feet, she moved over to stare down at the dead horse. Crouching down, she brought her hands in to one of the metal buckles of the saddle cinch, hooked her wrists onto the buckle and began sawing away. The ropes wet by the watery plunge refused at first to give way, then a strand went, and another, and then the rope gave way.

It took considerable more effort for Reba Jo to

remove the saddle from the dead horse floating on its side in the basin, and to get at the saddle blanket underneath. She smoothed out the saddle blanket on the rocky bank to let it dry, and then Reba Jo Cade took stock of her present situation.

"Can't be all that far into these mountains. But those outlaws . . . will they come down to see if I'm still alive . . .?

"Perhaps, as that cattle buyer didn't want any witnesses left behind . . ."

Her eyes swung downslope to the descending creek booming out watery sound. Then she studied the sky above the canyon in search of any more turkey vultures. What she hadn't heard while being held captive underneath that huge pool at the base of the cataract was the rattling of gunfire from above. What Reba Jo didn't know was that afterward the bodies of Shad Jarrett and three more outlaws had been shoved over the edge of the precipitous track passing deeper into the mountain. But what she was fully aware of was of her being unarmed and feeling the knife-edge pain coming from her lacerations.

"Dammit, woman, don't start feelin' sorry for yourself now. Night might be comin' on . . . but you've got that saddle blanket for a coat . . . and how about that hos's bridle for a weapon . . . ?" With both hands she brushed her dampened hair away from her face, she added bitterly, "At least those bastards didn't have their way with you."

It wasn't until a couple of days later that Brock Lacy learned of the Texan selling his horse and saddle. Then it was as if Guy Jarrett had disappeared only to have one of the outlaws catch a glimpse of Guy boarding a westbound train.

"You sure it was him?"

"Yup, Brock, as I had been this close from putting out his lights."

"You could'a," Lacy snarled, "been in the same shithouse with that Texan and plumb missed. West means he's headin' for Butte." Pondering this, Lacy got to wondering what the Texan had found out from Sheriff Taylor. Maybe Tysdale had been keeping some secret records of his dealings with the Divide Cattle Company. Something of this nature was Gavin Brazelton's worry, yet in this Lacy saw a chance to get a lot more dinero out of Brazelton. Anyway, he'd also found out that the sheriff had sent his deputies out looking for him and his hard cases.

"We're leaving."

"Back up to Commanche, Brock?"

"Not to that slim pickin' country. It'll be a new experience ridin' a train as a payin' passenger, boys. Butte, that's where we're headin' . . . to cut a deal with our old pal, Brazelton. So let's hustle out of this bar and find a buyer for our hosses."

Chapter Five

Mako Brazelton always felt a man was a fool to stop shaking the dice when they kept coming up winners. Behind him on the flats south of Butte lay one of his properties, a smelter whose towering smokestacks belched out sulfur smoke choking the sky over the city. Though he was dressed in the proper attire for a man about to attend a funeral, inwardly Mako Brazelton was smiling. He could scarcely believe Daphnie's father had passed away. Her mine owner father had less'n a week ago told Daphnie she would be disinherited unless she gave up on this idea of marrying Mako Brazelton. While she had gone into mourning, the last couple of nights had seen Mako sleeping over at a Silver Street bordello.

"Funny the way it works out," he said to his brother, Gavin, seated facing him in Mako's covered surrey passing uphill. "Here I had someone all lined up to take out Daphnie's old man."

"You still figure on gettin' hitched to her?"

"Expect I'll have to if I want to take over running the Dakota Mine. She's a saucy wench, but once a woman gets her hooks into a man . . . things change . . ."

"Joey settled down any?"

"Not so you'd notice," Mako said pensively. He flicked cigar ashes down, but careful so's not to get any on his black trousers. The easy living he'd found since venturing in here, and his bouts with hard liquor and the whores caused him to gain a little weight, which showed in his face. Recently he'd started working out at one of the local boxing clubs, where for a couple of rounds he'd held his own with an up and coming young pugilist, Spider Kelly. This mining camp, Mako had discovered to his delight, was a mecca for other sporting events. "Bought me a couple of fighters."

"And that mine, The Paradise Lady; heard it was about worked out —"

"Not for what I have in mind, Gavin."

"A grand scheme, Mako, if'n you don't run afoul of the law."

"That's where Judge Homer Rayburn comes in."

Most of the money the brothers Brazelton had received when they sold the stolen cattle had gone into buying the Empire Smelting Company. At first Gavin had been a reluctant partner, but even one so unschooled as Gavin Brazelton could envision a future as one of the copper kings, as Mako seemed to want to be. He squinted thoughtful eyes at Mako, said, "A lot different here than the Barbary Coast."

"A lot more money, for damned sure, Gavin."

Exhaling cigar smoke, Mako Brazelton studied the buildings spread over the richest hill in the world. Threading around the mines were the barren, gray mine dumps with faded cottages in clusters at their feet. Crooked dirt roads and

77

crumbling sidewalks led up the hill, most of the buildings of brick, a lot of unpainted framework, and around them sprouted huge steel and wooden gallows frames marking the entranceways to the mines. Ever since the smelters began operating to spew out sulfuric smoke not a blade of grass or a tree could be found in the city, Mako's impression of what he was viewing of a town centuries old.

But it was this town that would see Mako Brazelton making his fortune. Only two men knew of his scheme, and Gavin would keep what he knew to himself, and if Judge Homer Rayburn spoke of it, he'd wind up dead. Through Daphnie Coleman he expected to gain control of the Dakota Mine. The ore from the mine would be processed at his smelter, and even now Mako Brazelton was buying up property fringing onto the bigger mines. Soon he would have those he'd hired sinking prospect holes close to these paying mines, the shafts angling into the other mines, where his miners would purloin out ore. From here it was merely a matter of hoisting the ore to the surface and carting it off to Mako's smelter for processing. He expected his miners to be caught pirating copper ore, and litigation to be brought against him by the mine owners. Then Judge Rayburn would step in to make Mako Brazelton's transgressions legal. This would afford Mako precious time to take out more ore until months later the Montana Supreme Court reversed Rayburn's decisions. He expected strong-arm methods to be used against him, which could see a few getting killed. This was why he had his brother Gavin looking around to hire gunhands and bullyboys.

"Just give me a couple of years and I'll own this town."

"Appears you've got a good start already, Mako."

"Except for the chief of police—Jere the Wise is nobody's fool. But, that's my worry. What about back at Billings, did you leave any loose ends?"

"I told you about me exchanging telegrams with Brock Lacy."

"About this Texan coming in? So?"

"Cost me considerable, but last word I got from Lacy was he'd taken care of it. Along with gunning down a couple of others. Only thing is, Lacy's still there . . ."

"He knows your real name, you mean. Maybe you should head back over there and pay Brock Lacy a visit."

"Better yet, Mako, let's invite Lacy over here. Him and his boys could be hired on to use their guns if necessary."

"I get your drift, Gavin. Here we can keep an eye on Lacy. Then, if he gets ambitious . . ."

The man handling the reins was Mako Brazelton's personal bodyguard. Kiki Brown had been an out-of-work cowhand who'd drifted in to see what this mining town was all about. Only it chanced that he didn't cotton to mining, quit the Colusa Parrot Mine after one day of hacking at copper orc some sixteen hundred feet below the surface. The next day Brown got into a scuffle, which was Kiki Brown against three others. In the saloon at the time, the Big Stope, had been Mako Brazelton. With two plug-uglies stretched out at his feet, the onetime cowhand Brown was measuring another for the same treatment when the law arrived to cart Kiki Brown off to the city jail. That same afternoon Mako went over to post bail for Kiki Brown, and then offered him a job.

Unreposing at around five-ten, at Mako's insistence, Kiki Brown had discarded his cowboy garb in favor of a plain brown shirt though he still wore his high-heeled boots and the holstered Colt's. He was reining his team of matched blacks onto Gold Street when the word came for him to pull to the curbing.

Gavin Brazelton, emerging from the surrey, said to his brother, "Look, Mako, the kind of men you want me to hire want top dollar for their services. This ain't like out West."

"Okay, I'll loosen the purse strings. Though things are a mite tough at the moment. You sure you won't come to the funeral?"

"I didn't kill the sonofabitch . . . oh, pardon, the man who's gonna be your father-in-law. You still think marryin' her's a good idea?"

"As I hadn't bothered," smiled Mako, "to get divorced from the last one. Reckon Daphnie won't have it any other way. We'll get together tonight at the Council Bar. And if you run into Joey, pass the word I want to see him."

Gavin Brazelton was finding out that Butte was not one but two cities, one above and one below ground. The bulk of the miners were single, and foreigners, and living in boardinghouses in such sections of the city as Meaderville, Nanny Goat Hill, Seldom Seen, Dogtown, Chicken Flats, Butchertown, and Centerville. When viewed by night from the mountains Butte has been likened to a diamond set in jet. But daylight revealed this mining camp to be an uncorseted wench, dissipated from the night before, with a population of around forty thousand and growing.

The hulking Gavin Brazelton felt easier of mind when he prowled this town at night, as oftentimes he'd run into grifters and con men known to him. As for Mako wanting him to keep an eye out for their brother, it was Gavin Brazelton's notion that Jocy was more a nuisance than anything else—too damned reckless and uncaring. If it was him he'd send Joey packing.

Habit made him draw up in the dying shadows of twilight when a black police wagon trundled by just ahead of an ore wagon being drawn by an eight-span team of draft horses. He fished out a thick wooden toothpick and propped it in his mouth set to the sullenness of his mood. His mindset was more on the recent happenings in Billings, and the outlaw Brock Lacy. It was true Lacy and his men were gunhands, but to bring them here? Some of them were wanted for sundry crimes. What was it Mako had said, he wanted respectability. Explained further that the money he got out of copper would give him that, and more. "Guess money can buy a man most anything."

As for Gavin Brazelton, crime was all he'd known, and all he had ever wanted, to steal or kill. He was to be in charge of security for Mako's smelter, and those mines. Mako may pay out prime wages to the men taken on as security guards, but for damnsure they'd fork over part of their earnings to Gavin Brazelton. The thought chased away, at least momentarily, his worries about Billings.

Just as they'd done on the Barbary Coast, the Brazeltons had lined up a network of informers, some of them people employed by the mines or business places. Others Gavin forked out money to for information were the girls of the line, their pimps, and to panderers and procurers. He'd made the Comique his headquarters; a music hall located on South Main Street. Gavin Brazelton decided to head there instead of to the Butte Hotel for supper.

Rounding the corner onto Gold Street as mine whistles began sounding that it was six o'clock and quitting hour for the miners, he caught the eye of a man emerging from the Collar & Elbow Saloon. Roughly, Brazelton shoved by a peddler selling hot tamales from a handcart.

"Ah, Mr. Brazelton," said the man who'd just left the saloon, "You be headin' for the Comique?" He went by the name of Watts, and was one of the run-of-the-mill thugs hired by Gavin Brazelton. He wore nondescript clothing and an anxious smile.

"I hope you've got good news—"

"Just last night we took care of it, Mr. Brazelton," came his grinning response as he tried to match the other man's longer stride along the sidewalk. "That gambler won't be dealin' out pasteboards in this town again. Broke his thumbs, we did."

"About time," grumbled Gavin Brazelton. The gambler in question had sold him a few details about a certain mine owner that proved to be false. And by now the word of what had happened to the gambler would have spread. There was a sideways glance at Watts walking alongside. Men of his stripe liked to prowl in small packs along the dark alleys and byways of places like this and were more adept at rolling drunks or purse snatching than work involving gunplay, or murder. But they were a necessary evil, as were the whores, the gamblers and confidence men; the riffraff of every underworld from Corduroy Road in New Orleans to the Barbary Coast. One reason for his decision to bypass supper was that a certain gent was coming in on an afternoon train, the Utah and Northern narrow-gauge line connecting Butte to Ogden, Utah. What he knew of J. D. Valentine was sketchy, but this was the man Mako wanted.

"He'll have to prove out to me, too."

"Wha'cha say, Mr. Brazelton?"

"Watts?"

"Yup, Cedric Watts."

"Here." He thrust some paper money at the thug, and added, "I want you to contact your source over at the police station. Ask him what they've got on a J. D. Valentine—any paper out on him. Well, go do it."

There were two entrances to the Comique, the one off Main Street was for the common trade, but the one Gavin Brazelton always used was an entrance off the alley, as did the respectable element of Butte. He took in the music hall housed in a garish, two-story building, the ornate front patterned after the music halls of the East. A doorman lurked just inside the recessed doorway to chase any loiterers away, his careful eyes darting to Brazelton passing into the alley.

"Evening, sir."

Gavin Brazelton had the barest of shrugs for the man closing the back door. He took the staircase, emerged on the second-floor gallery, stall-like boxes encircling the walls to give those inside a view of the goings-on below. Each box was a separate compartment with an iron bolt on the inside of the door to ensure its user privacy. Completely covering the front of the boxes was a fine-mesh wire screen. Here those in the chips could raise hell, he mused, and if the truth be known, their depravities were worse than the common miner or blue-collar worker. Gavin knew, for a fact, as he'd been present when Mako had thrown a party for Butte aristocrats.

Again someone said good evening, but it was one of the waitresses scantily-clad in an evening dress. She opened one of the box doors, stood aside as Brazelton entered, to scowl out at her.

"There'll be two of us. Whiskey, an' be damned quick about it." He put his hat on the small table, settled onto the long bench and gazed down through the wire screen. The crowd was always the same, roughly garbed miners in here to spend hard-earned wages, the gamblers and diamond-bedecked bartenders and the women. No wall partitions separated the barroom from the auditorium, there were a few tables-for-four, and in progress on the stage was a vaudeville show. He knew word had spread of his presence up there.

Along with the waitress returning to pass through the open door came a nattily clad man nervously doffing his bowler hat. Waving the waitress away without bothering to add a tip to what he owed, Brazelton's hand gesture brought the stranger in to close the door. "Seems you work over at the Colusa Parrot?"

"Yessir, Mr. Brazelton. Emory . . . I mean I'm David Emory . . . a, an accountant . . ."

"So, what do you have?"

"We've hit a new vein of copper. You did mention some money if I . . ."

When occasion demanded, Gavin Brazelton could be charming, and a smile cut the frosty glint out of his pondering eyes. Through the smile he unpocketed his leather wallet, to extract some paper money which he let flutter onto the table. After that it was but a matter of moments before he had what he wanted from the accountant. After the accountant had taken his leave, others arrived to try and sell what they knew to Brazelton. He never tired of seeing men and women sell their souls and self-respect for a few miserly dollars. After a couple of hours of this, the noise from below rose a few octaves, and then a man he knew had to be J. D. Valentine was there, the pair of them regarding each other with speculating eyes.

What Gavin Brazelton took in was a tall and sparse man having all the earmarks of a gunfighter, though no holstered gun bulged out of Valentine's light brown coat. He had on faded Levi's and unspurred boots, a stoic set to his mouth. About the newcomer as he came into the box was an easiness of movement. He sat down across from Brazelton without waiting for an invite, and then poured whiskey into the spare shot glass.

"Cheers."

"How do you come to know Mako?"

"Don't."

Gavin Brazelton scowled. "Anyway, Mako and I talked over what we want you to do."

"I expect it has somethin' to do with minin', Mr. Brazelton." He downed the whiskey, grimaced. "Rough stuff."

"You want top-shelf stuff, you pay for it." He could feel Valentine's casual mannerism get to him, knew only what Mako had told him about the man. Gavin added, "How you heeled?"

"Not exactly busted, if that's what you mean. I was told my travelin' expenses would be picked up."

A nod from Gavin affirmed this. "Here's the way of it, Valentine. Me'n Mako ain't gunfighters but businessmen. Guns is where you come in."

He refilled the shot glass. "Just how does the law enter into what I'll be doing?"

"They've got a sonofabitch for a chief of police hereabouts."

"I know all about Jere the Wise. Not professionally; but word gets around."

"Well, you can slack off on the worry. As we've got a federal judge in our back pockets."

J. D. Valentine's eyes strayed through the screened wire mesh to take in the activity below. Without looking at the other occupant of the private box, he said quietly, "According to what I was told by Mako Brazelton's contact, I'll be more or less a troubleshooter."

"That, a hired gun, all the same. I expect it's been a long trip for you, Valentine. By the way, just where did you come from?"

Just barely above a whisper he said through a smile, "Utah an' Nevada . . . an' some other locales."

"Yeah, a troubleshooter." At that moment Gavin Brazelton couldn't help thinking of his dealings over at Billings and the outlaw Brock Lacy. More carefully he took in the green-gray tint to the eyes of the man seated facing him and the bronzed and somber face. He realized, finally, there was no way of actually knowing who'd be swifter at the draw, the man here or Lacy. Only way to find out was if Brock Lacy showed up in Butte.

"I learned a few things," came Valentine's southwestern drawl. "Since I pulled in this afternoon. One, there's a third brother, Joey, I was told. That you Brazeltons own a smelter and a mine."

"And?"

"And for damned sure you've got ambitions to add to this. And, Mr. Brazelton, I'm here in the capacity of professional gunfighter. Here to protect your vested interests." He pushed the shot glass full of whiskey away, and rose lithely. "I've got a room at the Finlen Hotel."

Alone, but with the presence of the gunfighter still hovering in the private box, Gavin Brazelton was impressed by one thing, in that Valentine hadn't asked for an advance payment for his services.

"Been around mining camps, he said. This might work out after all." But the nature of Gavin Brazelton cropped to the surface of his thoughts, a suspicion of the gunfighter until he'd proved up.

"Him taking out Lacy'll ease some of my worries."

He needed money, and he needed it desperately. Moreso for Joey Brazelton than ever before, which was Joey's reasons for heading over to the Montana Hotel in search of his brother, Gavin.

It wasn't the same here as out on the Barbary Coast, he'd found out to his dismay. His attempt to line up a string of whores had been stopped by Mako, as had a couple of other crooked ventures. "Mako's changed; maybe that damned mine owner's daughter has done it."

There were moments of confusion for Joey Brazelton, times when he got crazed, would lash out at his woman-of-the-moment, or there'd be blackouts. He rarely had a solid meal, but drank heavily, and gambled. Approaching the hotel from the south, his eyes held to his reflection in a front window, of a man whose clothes hung limply over a thinning frame and of a once-handsome face seemingly just flesh over bones.

Then he was inside the lobby, to be recognized by one of the desk clerks. "I believe your brother's out, Mr. Brazelton."

A bravado's smile appeared. "I know. But Gavin has some papers he wanted me to sign." Palming the room key, he headed jauntily to the staircase, slowed down on the second floor to get his wind back. "Should see a sawbones. But what the hell, probably just a cold or somethin'."

The key let him into a suite of rooms. And without wasting any time he went in to search the bedroom used by his brother by light filtering in through the windows from a street lamp. He mumbled impatiently as he opened yet another dresser drawer, "Gavin always keeps stuff laying around. Here, what's this?" In a bottom drawer his seeking fingers went under some socks and underwear to come in contact with a small box, and he lifted it out. Now, in his excitement of the moment, he set the box down on the bed and brought light to a lamp. He used the knife he always packed to break open the lock on the cherrywood box. He found the contents were more than he'd been looking for, for along with some paper money held in a gold money clip there was an assortment of jewelry, watches, the like. One piece of jewelry in particular caught the eye of Joey Brazelton.

He held it up to the light to murmur, "This is one necklace that'll dangle from around Sybil's pretty little neck." He'd first set eyes on Sybil over at the Alley Cat Saloon, a woman with black smoldering eyes and coal-black hair swirling around her bare shoulders. But to Joey's chagrined dismay, she'd scorned his advances, and this rankled him as all she was just a whore. Time and again he would head over to the Alley Cat, only to be rebuffed.

"But Sybil'll damnwell purr when she gets a gander at this necklace."

Joey Brazelton had no way of knowing his pilfering the abalone pearl necklace from his brother would set into motion a series of events that among other things would bring about his demise. All that mattered was the immediate need of getting some ready cash. Hurriedly he stowed the jewelry and money in his coat and trouser pockets, then replaced the cherry-wood box in the dresser.

Out on the night streets of the city, Joey Brazelton beelined for a pawn shop he knew would still be open with a new swagger in his step.

- "Sybil—that hussy an' me is about to have us some wild night . . ."

At last they were alone, in the front parlor of a mansion, a sadness for the events of this long day etched on Daphnie Coleman's face as she reached out for Mako Brazelton's hand. Willingly he came into her arms, to say comfortingly,

"Your father really loved you."

"Oh, Mako, if only you did . . ."

"But I do."

Her eyes flared open wider, and she gasped, "But . . . Oh, Mako, I love you so."

"I would have told you before, honey, but . . ."

"Yes, because of my father."

"I felt," he lied, "to do so wouldn't have been fair to you. That it would have put undo pressure upon you, honey. I hope you can understand?" He started to pull away.

"No, don't go. I don't want to be alone, not now."

"You have your servants—"

"I let them have the day off. This house . . . it's so big . . . seems so empty without my father around . . ."

He moved with her to a corner liquor cabinet, and she watched as he poured brandy into two glasses, and offhandedly he inquired, "The mine, what are your plans for it?"

"To keep it running, I suppose." Her fingers stroked his when Mako handed her the glass; a possessive gesture. "Mako, I'm at a loss when it comes to mining . . . but you, you own one, and a smelter, too."

"Daphnie, perhaps in a few days, when you're a little less sadder . . . we can discuss the Dakota Mine. From what I hear you've got a capable manager out there. Perhaps . . ."

"There's no perhaps about it, Mako. I've discussed my father's will with his lawyers. It's all mine, this house, the money, everything. All mine except you . . . my love . . ." Naked desire poured out of her eyes, and then she stepped over to put out the lamp. "I don't want to be alone tonight."

Reaching for her glass, he murmured huskily, "Neither do I."

Chapter Six

It didn't occur to Guy Jarrett until their passenger train was pulling into Butte that a day ago he'd turned thirty-four. With the remembrance of this came other things out of the past, and just for a moment he wondered if he'd erred in coming here. Those he loved and parded around with weren't here but dead and their bones scattered to the winds. And taking in the wide spread of this mining camp, Guy knew it would be a formidable task locating the cattle buyer.

Toting his lonely valise, he stepped down behind others viewing Butte and the western flanks of the Rockies for the first time, as was Guy. These people spoke a gibberish of foreign languages, and mostly they were men drawn in by the lure of mining copper. He noted the fact they'd come a heap farther than he had, and once they got acclimated out here, they would never go back.

"Lucky, as all they've got on their minds is finding a job."

He seemed to be the only cattleman pushing across the platform and on into the large depot. Wedging his way to the street fronting the Northern Pacific depot, one look upstreet told Guy it would be a long and dusty hike. He ducked into the backseat of a waiting transom hack.

"I'll be damned," the driver blurted out in an Irish brogue. "You're no foreigner. Seeing as you ain't, cowboy, I'll lower me rates."

"Gracías," Guy smiled as he began surveying the passing buildings. "Place is bigger'n I figured."

"She be that."

"The mines still hiring?"

"M'boy, they never stop hiring. But take me advice an' stay out of them damned mines."

He let the driver drop him off at a cut-rate hotel on Silver Street, went in to get a room. Afterward Guy Jarrett went in search of a local newspaper, a short jaunt that brought him just downstreet to the Cuba Cafe. From a passing paperboy he paid a nickel for the days edition of the *Butte Evening News,* then Guy found a booth in the small cafe. Over coffee he read the newspaper, took particular pains to study the business ads, on the off-chance there'd be some mention of the Divide Cattle Company. There wasn't, and somehow Guy expected this.

These hombres, he mused, were smart enough to cover their backtrail. On the train ride over from Billings he had put himself in the shoes of that cattle buyer, Falcone, and others who might be running this operation. He had concluded that from Billings on the stolen cattle had been consigned to a legitimate cattle company operating out of Butte. Now Guy had only a paper trail to follow, which he'd learned from his days as a Texas Ranger, often petered out damned quick. Guy grimaced his concern over this.

"Falcone; probably a bogus name, too. The

man's probably skipped out of here a long time ago."

The sheriff over at Billings had promised to keep in touch. Probably won't come up with anything, Guy mused. He took in a uniformed policeman strolling down the street, after he had been told by the driver of the hack that Butte had a large police force. But he felt to go to the police might tie his hands, as most probably they'd want to conduct their own investigation. And with what kind of evidence? If only his brother Wayland could tell him what happened. Grimly, he left coin on the table and departed the cafe.

The first couple of days found Guy Jarrett prowling the downtown streets, which always seemed to be thronged with pedestrians and vehicles. On every block there were at least half a dozen saloons, music halls, and gaming casinos, these places plying their trades next to grocery stores and haberdasheries. Brick buildings three- and four-stories tall had replaced the older wooden ones, though to Guy's eyes it was still a mining camp—open twenty-four hours a day. By late afternoon of his second day here, Guy reckoned he had been to all of the cattle companies having downtown offices.

Renting a horse, he set it cantering along wide and downsloping Broadway Street. The sky was tarred with low-moving smoke coming from smelters, the acrid stench of it not to his liking. There on the lower slope of the hill the houses were packed together, a lot unpainted, and here and there picket fences guarding barren front yards. A forlorn place to raise a family, he felt. Out of one house came a woman, slim and young, brought her hand to brush a strand of yellow-colored hair away from her face

94

with a graceful movement so much like Reba Jo's that Guy had to force his eyes away. When he glanced back, she was gone, and he felt lonelier than ever.

"Well, here's the train depot," he muttered impatiently, and Guy swung the gelding onto a rutted side street. The holding pens he passed were empty, farther on though he came upon some holding cattle. He took in the brands and ear notches, noted without thinking too much about it the condition of the cattle, as any cattleman would. Uptown, he was told of three cattle companies having offices out here—the red sign with black printing off to his right and over a doorway of a frame building—Empire Cattle Company.

"Owned by a man named Gainsforth. An' a squareshooter, according to downtowners." Tying up, he planted his boots on the front porch steps, stepped up and inside, the screen door closing behind Guy announcing his presence.

"Back here."

He bypassed a front office to go back there, which he discovered was a back room occupied by four men engaged in a game of cut-throat pinochle. Right away a roly-poly man in a pin-striped suit caught his eye, and Guy paused to tip his hat back and shape a smile. "Mr. Gainsforth?"

"Well, here's someone with a common bond. Meaning its been a spell since any ranchers have come in. Grab that empty chair over there, Mr . . ."

"Guy Jarrett."

"And drag it over. Ignore the cards, Mr. Jarrett, as this is a sales meeting." A chuckling smile puffed out the man's ruddy cheeks. "My associates, Bell, Targhee, Collier. So, did you have cattle to sell?"

"Did have back about a year ago." He spread his hands out, added, "Do you mind if we have a private talk?"

"No, no, s'matter of fact." He pulled out a big round watch. "About quitting time anyway. You boys be here around six, as it'll take most of the day to get out to the XL ranch." As the other card players rose and headed out of the room, the cattle buyer, Gainsforth, gathered up the spread of playing cards and set them to one side. "Don't see many Texans up here"

"Can't fool anybody as to where I came from. Last year I expect you must have seen a bunch of Texans up here."

"Did indeed, Mr. Jarrett."

He picked up the stub of pencil lying next to the sheet of paper the card players had used to keep score, and then Guy turned it over to draw the J-J brand, the Circle C, and the two other brands, and quietly he asked, "It would have been late last summer, that cattle bearing these brands were brought in here."

"Gotta tell you, Mr. Jarrett, I was bedridden a lot last year. But business went on as usual. But that Circle C brand . . . could have seen it. But, here . . ." He stood up and moved over to a wooden cabinet, began pawing through paperwork in the top drawer. "Yup, sales slips for July, August." Lifting out two manila folders, he set them before Guy on the worn tabletop.

"I see other Texas outfits came in. Braddock; got an outfit west of me." Handing one manila envelope back to Gainsforth, Guy opened the other one, but the result proved to be the same, and he looked up. "Nothing."

"Like I said, I was gone a lot."

"Who was in charge when you were gone?"

"Collier — or sometimes it was Targhee. Known both men a long time, so I reckon these records are accurate as to what cattle we bought."

"I suppose so," Guy replied. "Ever hear of the Divide Cattle Company?"

"Nope, no such outfit here in Butte."

"Or a man named Neal Dunwoody; came down to Texas wanting to buy cattle. Or someone else . . . a man operating out of Billings . . . big man, fancy dresser, called himself Deal Falcone."

"Both names don't ring any bells. There is something, though." He let Guy rise, then he added, "Could be just wild stories, too. Us cattle buyers get together on occasion to swap lies and such. I guess it boils down to that there were times when Texas livestock arrived here in Butte but nary a sign of the owners. Got cattle buyers over at Billings, too, but all the same . . ."

Guy could read character better'n most, and concluded that cattle buyer Gainsforth was telling the truth as he knew it. He masked his disappointment behind a patient smile, though he could see questions dancing in the cattle buyer's eyes. To tell Gainsforth the grisly details of all that had happened would serve no purpose. The others who'd been here, Bell, Targhee, Collier, though just hirelings, did have access to the records on the table. Though the trio of them had been decked out in cattlemen's clothing, it was unlikely any of them had worked on a ranch. When Guy left, it was to climb into the saddle and rein the gelding eastward along the railroad right-of-way. Farther on he came to another cluster of buildings wedged in near holding pens, only to find the office of the Mountain Cattle Company locked up for the night. A groaning noise ushered through the spreading darkness, and the horse fought the bit, but Guy knew it was another ore wagon going downhill toward the smelters.

He found his way back to the train depot and lower Broadway. From behind along the holding pens came another horseman. Jake Targhee held his horse to a walk, as he didn't want to get in too close to the Texan. The unexpected appearance of Guy Jarrett breaking up their pinochle game was something that Targhee knew would happen sooner or later, be it this Texan or another one. Targhee was lean and hatchet-faced, with a middle-aged spread. All he knew was the selling game, cows or coffins or ladies' unmentionables, he'd done it.

It had been Buzz Collier who'd gotten him involved in this scam of Gavin Brazelton's. What the hell though, mused Jake Targhee, we made a bundle out of it. The cattle they'd bought from Brazelton they'd sold to the stores and restaurants of Butte. Targhee and Collier's part in it, had been to doctor the books of the cattle company simply by destroying a lot of sales slips involving Texas cattle. Over the winter he'd put to bed any worries about his involvement. But they sprang up anew when the Texan showed, and after leaving the building there'd been a brief discussion about this with Buzz Collier, only to have Collier clap him on the back and say,

"What can that damned Texan find out, Jake? We're clean. Just drop it."

But Jake Targhee hadn't been able to as he'd slipped around to find an open window, the words of the Texan a damning indictment of what he'd

98

done. Standing there in the first traces of twilight, questions began triphammering through his mind, as to how Gavin Brazelton had acquired the cattle, the names of others who might be involved, just what to do about the Texan.

"Dammit," muttered Jake Targhee upon swinging northward on Broadway Street, "just what did that Texan want? It's what he didn't say that bothers me." And then the response of his boss, Ben Gainsforth, in wondering why the owners of these cattle hadn't shown up in Butte. "All I know is the cattle were shipped here from Billings. Beyond that . . ."

The man having the answers to these questions turned the gelding in at the livery stable, the hostler grumbling that the horse should have been brought back before this. But engrossed in his thoughts, Guy Jarrett had moved away in the direction of his hotel.

How many trail herds were stolen? How many other bodies littered that killing graveyard down by the Crow Reservation? Despite all the activity on the bustling downtown street, Guy had never felt more aloof, as though he were a social outcast. He thought, looked beyond the stolen cattle, everything else, those cattle buyers thereabouts, maybe to a deeper reason. It hadn't just been some cattle rustlers. Cattle buyers had come down to Texas, as part of a well-conceived operation. There were thousands of dollars involved here, money that would never reach its rightful owners in Texas.

"It'll take time," pondered Guy as he veered over to give a bunch of miners direct access to a saloon. Beyond, his pace picked up again, with his hotel just upstreet, and with Guy Jarrett of a mind to get some supper. A man, he realized, couldn't survive for long on two scanty meals a day. "And the way prices are here, job hunting is another priority."

Drawing up farther downstreet, Jake Targhee held to the shadows as the Texan went into the Overland Hotel. He pulled out his handkerchief and doffed his hat, began wiping the sweat away from the inner hatband, his eyes lidded with uncertainties. "Drop it, Collier said?" Perhaps, mused Jake Targhee, just pulling back is the smart thing. But that's where the difference came in, as Buzz Collier never took things seriously, or ever expressed a solid opinion about anything. The fast buck was Collier's long suit. As for that other cattle buyer, he'd found out his name wasn't Falcone but Brazelton.

Worriedly he muttered, "Yup, don't ever want to cross this Gavin Brazelton. There's a brother, too, bought that smelter. Bar talk is of them being heavy hitters, killers. Damn, wish this Texan hadn't showed."

With a worried baring of his yellowed teeth against the deeper swarthiness of his face, cattle buyer Jake Targhee took all that was troubling him into a nearby saloon. Sometimes all of a man's problems came home to roost. It didn't sink in until the fourth or fifth glass of corn whiskey that he could turn a profit over this.

"Best thing is . . . leave Collier out of this. Just make a deal with Brazelton. Still . . ." Warning vibrations told Targhee to lay off the whiskey and plumb forget this notion, but he held to the chair, a hand rising to fetch a barmaid over, his worry now that someone else might tell Brazelton of that Texan coming in.

100

Chapter Seven

A day after his marriage to Daphnie Coleman, the ambitious Mako Brazelton was not only back at work but he'd taken over the Dakota Mine. From an office window he gazed past the Butte Brewery Building to the hill pockmarked with mines. The suit he wore, a black double-breasted, was a present from his new wife, along with the diamond tiepin. He should have been in a mellow frame of mind. But on his desk were papers served just this morning by a deputy sheriff.

The office was a mahogany-walled cavement patterned after that of copper king Marcus Daly's, but pretentiously larger. The one large window let in sunlight from the north. There was a patent-leather coach and two chairs, the oaken desk, and other office furniture. The door to the connecting bathroom stood open, to reveal another door which opened into a bedroom Mako often used.

Mako turned away from the window to regard the painting on the wall above the liquor cabinet. It was a seascape of a stretch of wharf backgrounded by a city. It had been propped in the front window of a Gold Street pawn shop when Mako had chanced by. The painting was Mako's sordid past.

To him it symbolized the pitfalls of the Barbary Coast, and that it didn't hurt a man to look back over his shoulder at times to see how far he'd come. He keened an ear to the sounds filtering into the room, of men and machinery at work in his smelter. The sobering fact that the smelter was processing copper ore pilfered from the Mountain Consolidated Mine wasn't disturbing to Mako Brazelton. The mine was just another Anaconda property owned by Marcus Daly.

"The copper king . . ." A cocky smile went with Mako as he settled in behind his desk. "Has started legal proceedings." He picked up the summons, a writ of assistance, a legal device that gave officers of the court authority to snoop about his mining properties. Carelessly, he deposited the summons in a desk drawer as he heard his secretary say,

"Yes, Mr. McLean, you're expected."

Mako reached to open the humidor and when Con McLean strode into his office, a flip of Mako's wrist sent a cigar twirling through a ray of morning sunlight. Deftly, McLean caught the cigar and said, "You seem damned chipper this mornin', Mr. Brazelton . . ."

Pushing to his feet, Mako lit his cigar, then brought the match across the desk to bring flame to McLean's. He liked Con McLean's caustic attitude, and like him, the man's past was open to question. In his role as manager of Mako Brazelton's mines, McLean had proved out far better than others Mako had hired for the job. McLean was big and brawny, had to be to control both his foremen and the hard-drinking miners. Sweat and copper silt stained his dark blue shirt. He had a face burned dark as old leather, and was clean-shaven. Dragging in cigar smoke, he began unrolling the map he'd brought along on the desktop.

"You know," he said conversationally, "we got a lot of ore out before those Anaconda people caught wind of it."

"Just got served with a summons," grinned Mako. "The judge's worry now . . ."

"Hope so," McLean said, jabbing a finger at the plat map of the city and surrounding land. "The Dakota Mine; not all that much high-grade ore taken out of it."

"But consider where it's located, Con." His eyes threw out a dreamy glint. "Here's the Anaconda."

"What Daly considers his top-payin' mine?"

"The Dakota is sandwiched between Mr. Daly's Anaconda and Paycheck mines. Here, here, and here, Con, my agents have very quietly bought up these vacant lots, a couple of businesses . . ."

Con McLean's character trait was to never allow the niceties of a smile, nor did McLean ever pass out compliments to men working for him, things he considered signs of weakness. He had gotten what he called "raw deals" from a couple of Copper City mines, but it was his drinking and shaking down of men under his command that had caused Con McLean to be given pink slips.

When the offer of a job had come from Mako Brazelton, he'd sized up Brazelton as being a brazen con man. At the saloon he hung out and at other low dives McLean had pieced together what some would consider an ugly picture of the Brazelton brothers. Ambitious, unscrupulous, not above taking out someone bold enough to cross them — these were things with which McLean had familiarity. Considered also by Con McLean was his burning

103

desire to strike back at those he'd once bossed miners for, that damned Anaconda bunch. His eyes holding to the map, McLean said cagily,

"They know you've taken over the Dakota Mine—"

"Certainly, Mr. McLean. But . . ." Mako's hand swept up along the crosscutting lines of the map. "I've purchased two more mines."

A lot more interest flared in Con McLean's eyes as he muttered ponderingly, "The Jasmine and the Tenderloin; never heard they were for sale."

"My name won't be registered as owning them. But own them I do, Con." Mako sat down on the edge of the desk, flicked burning embers from his cigar into an ashtray. "For now, we'll play it straight at the Dakota Mine. Here, the Tenderloin—abutting it the Neversweat—a lot of Mr. Daly's high-grade ore coming out of it, which I want."

"Daly'll be pissed, for damned sure." He turned, gazed out the window uphill at smokestacks issuing clouds of grayish smoke. "Him, Daly and Clark think they own this town. You shouldering-in says different."

"You worried?"

"Mostly I'm just thinkin' of the future of a certain Con McLean." He said it without malice, but the meaning was clear to Mako Brazelton.

"Can't blame a man for being ambitious. An' can't afford to have you go elsewhere, Con. Together we can make this thing work."

"What about your brothers?"

Mako laughed. "They're involved in other things besides mining."

Con McLean knew all about the things Mako Brazelton's brothers were involved in, especially that

104

Gavin. Here was a man he tried to avoid whenever possible. They'd, him and Mako, discussed just what mines to try and buy, one of them being the Tenderloin. Until his untimely death less'n a month ago the man owning the Tenderloin had publicly stated his hatred of Mako Brazelton. Then he was dead; died in his sleep, according to the Silver Bow county coroner. Foul play in the form of the Brazeltons was behind it, McLean knew with a grim certainty. But those copper kings didn't gain their high status by not taking a few risks, and maybe including murder. Getting access to high-grade ore meant taking high risks.

"About the Tenderloin . . ."

"I know, not a high producer. Some time back, couple of months ago, I received a visit from an Anaconda engineer. That visit cost me five thousand dollars, and the reason I bought the Tenderloin. Here, in the Neversweat, there's an immense body of ore only this engineer knows about."

"The Neversweat's a big mine," pondered McLean. "What quality of ore we talking about?"

"Forty, fifty percent copper ore. That vein of ore lays close to the northern boundary lines of the Tenderloin. Its tailor-made for us, Con. Somewhere in the neighborhood of a hundred thousand tons of ore."

"We'll have to hire more men, for sure. By the by, Mako, you were speakin' of givin' my boys a pay raise . . ."

"They'll see that increase on this Friday's paychecks. And I'm also going to cut the daily work hours from ten to eight; which is what the unions want anyway."

"Nothin' like gettin' the men on your side." Con

McLean made no comment as the man he worked for passed over a thick yellow envelope, though a glance inside revealed it contained one-hundred-dollar bills.

"That's just for starters, Con. Just to show you that we appreciate all you've done. How soon can you get going over at the Tenderloin?"

"I expect tomorrow morning. And obliged, Mako."

After the departure of the general manager of his mining enterprise, coffee was brought in to Mako Brazelton, who busied himself with office routine. It pleased him to buy the loyalty of men such as Con McLean, and it didn't hurt either that McLean had a score to settle with his former employers. A different matter of concern was the arrival of J. D. Valentine, the gunfighter. You didn't buy his loyalty but his gun. The bargaining chip for the gunfighter was cash on the barrel head, then he went out to kill without remorse, moved on to kill again. A professional, as Mako Brazelton felt he was.

Plopping a couple of lumps of sugar into his cup, Mako stirred his coffee about as he went over in his thoughts the unexpected demise of the owner of the Tenderloin Mine at the hands of the gunfighter, J. D. Valentine. And smooth as silk, grinned Mako. Gunning down the mine owner, he had explained to Valentine, might bring about a long criminal investigation or see the ownership of the mine tied up in court. The way the killing went was the gunfighter going to the mine owner's house a long ways after midnight. The gunfighter found under the goose-down quilt in the big bed the mine owner emitting snores and his wife equally asleep. Undismayed by the presence of the woman, Valen-

106

tine had used a pillow to suffocate the mine owner. Then he left as quietly as he'd come.

"Mr. Brazelton, ah, your brother is here—"

"Ah, send him in."

But Gavin Brazelton had already thrust himself past the secretary and strode up to the desk without bothering to remove his hat. "We've got a problem."

Mako didn't respond until the secretary had closed the office door, and then he nodded to have Gavin Brazelton blurt out, "That damned Lacy bunch is in town."

"Your friends over at Billings? Fancy that?"

"Dammit, Mako, this means trouble for us."

"In that he wanted more money, or else?"

"About it, dammit." Now Gavin Brazelton pulled off his hat and slammed it down on the desk as he slumped into a chair, "Valentine, what we've got him here for . . ."

"Yeah, if it comes to that. What about Joey . . ."

"He's your brother, too, dammit, Mako. I'm tired of wet-nursing that runt . . . half-drunk all the time . . ." He rubbed at his nose. "That coffee any good?"

"Yeah," Mako said with a weary sigh, "I'll see you get some." He rose to move over and crack open the door, and found his secretary talking to someone who seemed vaguely familiar, "Alice, another cup of coffee. Yes . . . yes, you're Targhee, a cattle buyer."

"I told him you were busy, Mr. Brazelton. If you will have a seat, Mr. . . ."

"No, don't sit down, Mr. Targhee. Come on in, and Alice, make that two more cups of coffee." Waving Targhee ahead of him, Mako knew the presence of Jake Targhee meant trouble for him. Most of the dealings with that Butte cattle company had been handled by Gavin. And perhaps, as Gavin had suggested at the time, both Targhee and the other cattle buyer, Buzz Collier, should have been sent packing. Retaining the pleasant smile, Mako gestured toward the other chair before his desk. "Haven't seen you for a spell, Jake. Still working out there?"

"Can't shake a bad habit, I reckon. Wouldn't have bothered coming out here . . . but something's come up . . ."

"Such as?" spat out Gavin.

"Easy," Mako murmured to his brother, "I'm sure Jake has his reasons for coming here—"

"Truth is, I'm damned worried. Plumb forgot about our business dealings until this hombre shows up. A Texan, Mr. Brazelton, an' askin' a lot of questions."

"What did you tell this . . . Texan?"

"Wasn't me nor Collier talkin' to him. We left the Texan with my boss, Gainsforth. I snuck around to a window and listened in, though. Afterward, I followed the Texan to where he's camped out at an uptown hotel. Still there, too."

"Is this it?"

"Not quite," blustered Jake Targhee. "All I want is to bail out of this mining camp an' not come back, for damned sure, Mr. Brazelton."

"But that takes money—"

"A heap, I reckon. A couple of thousand should do it, to have me tell you boys where to find the Texan, for me to skedaddle." His nervous eyes took in the secretary coming in bearing a tray, but he waved the coffee away, as Mako said,

108

"A couple of thousand sounds reasonable, Mr. Targhee. A check or . . ."

"Cash'll do." He scrambled to his feet as Mako Brazelton fished out his wallet. Scarcely had the money been counted out and was in his hand than the cattle buyer was shying out of the office.

The hand that shoved Mako's wallet back into an inner-coat pocket was rigid with anger. He brought the hand out to point it at his brother. "You were right."

"Want my boys to handle it? Or Mr. Valentine?"

"Nope, since Brock Lacy is in town he just might be looking for work . . ."

"Lacy? All he came here for was to shake us down!"

"You forget the lessons learned on the Barbary Coast, brother of mine. Sure, Lacy came here expecting a big payday."

"Why he didn't kill that Texan back at Billings I'll never know, Mako. Five of them and one broken-backed rancher; don't make no sense. What do you make of it?"

"This Texan, came up looking for his kinfolk and to find out just what happened to his cattle. I want him taken care of, Gavin, and Targhee and that other cattle buyer, Collier. What I don't want is anybody tracing it back here. Do I make myself clear?"

"Why you getting your hackles up at me, dammit, Mako?"

"Not you so much. Just blaming myself for not taking out these cattle buyers before, as you suggested. Too, there's so much at stake here, Gavin. Millions—a new life for the Brazeltons."

"Okay, okay, I get your drift, Mako. From here on in we let others do our dirty work."

"More or less," he smiled. "Keep on with what you've been doing. Up there, Gavin, you're getting the pulse beat of what's going on better'n me out here. We'll need more security for those mines I've bought. But for now, find Brock Lacy and lay it out to him. Might even wine and dine his bunch."

"What about you showin' up to pour that wine . . . ?"

"My new bride won't let me out at night."

Gavin Brazelton laughed and said, "Yeah, you do look a little peaked at that."

"I guess that's it for now. Just see that Texan's occupying a grave plot, an' those others."

"Afterward?"

"Brock Lacy you mean — claims to be a gunslinger. Be interesting to see him stacked against a real gunhand. Real interesting . . ."

Chapter Eight

Just upstreet from Guy Jarrett's hotel was the Big Stope Bar. By now he could count how many steps it took for him to get over there, or to other saloons as he went about searching for that cattle buyer. What troubled him most of all was that nobody in Butte had ever heard of the Divide Cattle Company. He'd been forced to resole his high-heeled boots, and reshape his thinking about what to do next.

Yesterday a letter had arrived from Billings in response to one Guy had sent to the sheriff over there. About all the letter Guy had received told of the outlaw Brock Lacy pulling out. At least when he was a Texas Ranger there'd been others toting badges. You'd think, he mused bitterly and as he strode along the crowded sidewalk under a darkening sky, that something would break.

And what was breaking Guy Jarrett were the high prices hereabouts. Nobody seemed to be complaining, especially the miners, as during these boom times they were working seven days a week. A man couldn't help falling into conversation with a miner since the saloons were a miner's second home. Guy had learned that all anyone had to do to be hired on was to be able to suck air into his lungs. The risks were high though, as these men toiled below at depths up to two thousand feet. Pausing upon arriving at an intersection, he pulled in close to the wall of the Big Stope saloon to take out the Durham and papers. While shaping a cigarette, he took in the bedlam of the street.

One thing he'd learned about Butte was of it being a city of horses. The mines, the smelters, breweries, a host of other businesses, employed horses of varying shapes and sizes. There were the dog-eaters or Cree and the Chippewa—Indian tribes camping out on the flats near the city dump with their ponies. Coming into town on occasion were cowhands on saddle broncs, and still competing with the railroads were a couple of stagecoach outfits.

"Could hire on as a stagecoach driver," Guy murmured silently. "Or there's this gent Turner breaking horses just east of town. But don't crave gettin' busted up in that line of work."

It came to him then where he stood idling a few feet from a narrow walkway passing between the saloon and the next building lining the street, a furtive voice saying,

"I tell you we should do it when that damned Callahan leaves the Big Stope."

"Look, Sheldon, I'm not payin' you to think. That bastard Callahan just won't leave my woman alone. Damned if she ain't favorin' him more'n me. I want him dead, Sheldon, by your knife or mine . . . all and the same."

"He could hang in there all night."

"Which is why I'm gonna flush that bastard out

112

of there. He'll think it'll be just him and me at rough and tumble over my woman. Callahan's a hotheaded sonofabitch, so it won't take much to head him out the back door. Now, Sheldon, that's where you come in . . ."

"We checked it out before an' there ain't no light out back. So just make sure Callahan comes out first as I might carve you up instead, Mr. Pierce."

Up on the sidewalk, Guy Jarrett swung over to shove into the saloon. He knew the miner in question, a gregarious Irishman named Muggy Callahan. The bulk of the men coming in here to work in the mines weren't married, and if they were, they never revealed this to the army of girls plying their trade along Venus Alley or working in the night spots of the city. It didn't take Guy long to spot the lanky and work-clad Irishman hoisting a stein of beer at one of the many tables, and he went there.

"Me boys, it's the man from Texas come to join us as we drown our sorrows in drink. There, Murphy, drag that chair over for Mr. Jarrett."

There was a shifting of chairs by the others to make room for Guy's chair at the table. Easing onto it, he nudged Callahan's arm to say quietly, "A man named Pierce will be dropping in shortly."

Blinking in puzzlement, the miner replied, "Pierce, you say?"

"Claims you've been courting his girlfriend."

"Oh, that Mr. Pierce. A lowlife if ever there was one, Mr. Jarrett. The truth of the matter is . . . here, there's plenty of beer to go around . . . the truth is Pierce's girlfriend likes to roam around. All over town, I've heard. Me, nah, just because I bought the fair lass a few glasses of spirits . . ."

"He isn't alone as Pierce's confederate will be waiting out back just to ventilate your belly, Mr. Callahan. And there enters our Mr. Pierce. Hmmm, awful runty for a man wanting to challenge you to fisticuffs." Guy shoved to his feet, and added, "Believe I'll take a stroll out back."

Threading through the tables, Guy flicked a disinterested glance at the one called Pierce in passing, then he was outside and cutting around to the side walkway. Quickly he passed along it, with a spare gun he always packed along tucked into his waistband. From what he'd overheard, the man out back favored a knife, and would be centering his attention on the backdoor. Which proved to be the case when Guy eased around to the back wall, and saw him palming the .36-caliber Allen & Wheelock. The blurred movement of Guy's arm was followed by the thud of his revolver hitting bone and flesh, and the one known as Sheldon folded to the ground.

"Should be interesting what happens next," smiled Guy as he held out there. Across the alleyway was a maze of back windows in buildings fronting onto the next street. A few windows were framed in light, and Guy had to half chuckle at a miner trying to wrap his arms around a woman of ample proportions. Farther along and in the next building a man was folded over an open window and retching out the contents of his stomach. He'd been in some hard-drinking towns before, but Butte was a topper, the vast horde of miners seeking their pleasures every day of the week and damned near around the clock.

114

Exploding out of the backdoor of the Big Stope came Muggy Callahan. Callahan pulled up in the mud and gumbo of the alleyway and threw himself around, one hand jamming his hat down hard, the other gesturing impatiently at the man just stepping outside. "So, Mr. Pierce, as you can see I'm not packing a weapon."

Pressed in against the back wall, Guy could see the uncertainty playing across Pierce's face where he stood outlined in light pouring out of the open door. Blinded by the inner lights of the tavern, Pierce spat out, "No dirty sidewinder is gonna steal my woman." He came out farther, wanting to go for the knife tucked into his belt as Callahan shuffled toward him with his fists primed for action.

"Its just you and me, Pierce. Unless you were expecting someone to back up your play . . ."

"No, damn you, Callahan, I . . ." Finally his groping eyes landed upon Guy Jarrett lurking in the shadows. "Dammit, Sheldon, get in behind the bastard!"

"Sheldon. No, I'm not Sheldon. Believe he's taking a nap at the moment." Guy eased away from the wall and into reflecting light.

With a vengeful smile glued to his face, Muggy Callahan threw a lusty right-hand punch. The head of his assailant snapped back. Then the miner gazed down in contempt at the man he'd knocked out. He laughed boisterously, his thick Irish brogue coming to Guy in a friendly way,

"That was no fight, me friend. But did you see his eyes, Mr. Jarrett, all bulging out with fear when you spoke out. The rub is Pierce is still

115

alive. As he belongs to a gang of thugs; sames the other one. These scum prey upon the downtrodden, muggings and knifings and such. It just could be they'll be coming after you, as you spoiled their fun."

"Could be. What about them?"

"Attempted murder is a serious charge. We could call the law — but a waste of time as Pierce's friends will bail him out. So come now, me friend, as Muggy Callahan is treating you to a night on the town."

That night on the town found Guy Jarrett unloading some of his thoughts to the miner Callahan. He learned a lot, too; that men were needed at the mine where Muggy Callahan worked, and that the criminal underworld operated here in Butte. Early the next morning Guy checked out of the hotel without leaving a forwarding address. He found new lodging at the Florence Hotel, affectionately known to the miners as the "Big Ship", and home to Callahan and about a hundred other men toiling in the mines. At breakfast, Guy sat alongside Callahan in the large dining room. They ate a couple of bowls of gruel from the stirabout pot. Afterward, he purchased work boots and clothing, and then Guy set off on foot with Callahan for the Neversweat Mine.

Through breaking clouds still unloading rainwater Guy Jarrett got his closest look at the inner yard of a working copper mine. The ground was barren, the buildings rambling affairs coated with silt but otherwise in good shape. Slag heaps set to glistening by the rain lay deeper in the mine yard, the pounding of a steam engine coming from near the two-decker gallows frame. Thick black smoke merged cloudlike above the Neversweat's seven towering smokestacks. Below and above other mines, some not as large as the Neversweat, dotted the barren hillscape.

Curiosity prompted Guy to ask, "Why do they call it the Neversweat?"

Muggy Callahan, shoving open a door passing into what appeared to be the mine office, threw back, "Hard as the work is down in a mine a man'll never sweat." He had a smile for a man seated at a desk. "And a good morning to you, Shawn O'Leary."

"Callahan, its too early in the morning to listen to your blarney."

"But, Shawn, I'm here with good reason. May I present a man able to speak the King's English. This be Guy Jarrett out of the Republic of Texas."

"Jarrett, huh? All I can say is you're in bad company. So, is it a job you're wanting? Or a handout?"

Guy decided as he stepped closer to the desk that O'Leary's sharp tongue of the moment was just a cover, that he and Callahan were friends. Quietly Guy replied, "A job sounds good right about now."

"I'm certain, Mr. Jarrett, the prospect of working in a copper mine didn't bring you out of Texas."

"Nossir," he said, "it sure didn't. But sometimes a man gets down on his luck."

"You've got that look as being a man used to

117

the wide open spaces. We use a lot of horses and mules, could use someone like you to work around them."

"O'Leary, you insult me friend Jarrett simply by asking him to work behind a mule. A man's work is what he's after, doing same as me."

"Callahan, Mr. Jarrett can speak for himself."

"Mining, I'll give it a go," said Guy.

"Then you're hired." O'Leary scribbled some words on a pad, to tear away the top sheet and hand it to Guy. "Give that to your shift boss. Callahan here will see you're outfitted with a safety lamp and helmet . . . and good luck, Jarrett."

It wasn't until he was outside and coming onto the entrance to the mine marked by a steel gallows frame that Guy thought to ask, "Just how far down are we going?"

"We'll be working at the eleven-hundred-foot level," said Muggy Callahan as he went ahead into the cage with other miners.

Then an apprehensive Guy Jarrett entered the cage. The cage operator closed the heavy iron door and with a humming of gears and cables the cage was suddenly plunged below. Too soon they were at the designated level of the mine and leaving the cage, with the lights from their safety helmets guiding the miners along one of the drifts shored up with timbers. Guy didn't particularly like going into caves in the first place, the sense of eeriness about the mine took hold of him. But to keep on looking for that cattle buyer he needed money to survive on, be it working down here at the Neversweat or at some other job.

"Here's the stope where we'll be toiling away,

Mr. Jarrett. Our shovels are in that empty ore car." He had a wide smile for Guy, which Callahan now shared with the other miners. "I think Mr. Jarrett's color is comin' back, boys. So, let's bend to gettin' at that copper ore."

The night clerk at the Overland Hotel barely had time to let out a frightened whimper before Brock Lacy's leather quirt struck the back of his hand. "Where did the Texan go, dammit?"

"Just . . . he just checked out . . . I swear . . ."

At a nod from Brock Lacy the two men holding the clerk threw him back onto a chair behind the counter and Lacy said stonily, "You go to the law with this and I'll cut out your tongue. Come on, we're wasting our time here."

The outlaws tramped out of the hotel, where Brock Lacy headed in the direction of the Big Stope Saloon in a swaggering walk. He'd come here with the intentions of blackmailing Gavin Brazelton, only to have Brazelton talk him into taking on the job of killing three men. Not that this displeased Brock Lacy. More had been said in their conversation, in that just maybe if this was handled right, there'd be other jobs for Lacy and his men.

"Maybe it was just as well we didn't take out the Texan back at Billings."

"Brock, you sure we can trust Brazelton . . . ?"

"Trust, nope, I don't trust him. Just that he needs us to do his dirty work."

They'd been given not only the name of the hotel where the Texan was supposed to have taken up lodging, but just where they could find that pair of cattle buyers, Targhee and Collier. Through his Butte connections, Brock Lacy had learned quite a deal about the Brazelton brothers and their ambitious plans. To his surprise the blood-wiping money gained from selling the stolen cattle had been used by the Brazeltons to purchase mining property. "Those bloodsuckers have got themselves a smelter and some mines. An' this son of hell is gonna get his share out of it. Or to the law I'll be goin'."

Along with Brock Lacy, three other hard cases had decided to come along to Butte. The pair straggled to either side, and Red Kiely was detailed to keep tabs on one of the cattle buyers. At last report Jake Targhee was snuggling in with one of the damsels plying her trade in a Venus Alley crib. The other one, Collier, would be shuffling a deck of cards someplace; from what the man's landlady had told Brock Lacy. There was the urge in Lacy, as he came abreast of the Big Stope Saloon, to stop in for a drink as he could afford that and a lot more with what Gavin Brazelton had given him. But he held to the street, the new knee-length cattleman's coat concealing his holstered Colt's, though anyone chancing to return his glance would know this was no ordinary cowhand in for a good time.

Something that a man idling across the busy street knew, as J. D. Valentine also knew where the outlaws were headed. Valentine had been told to keep an eye on Brock Lacy by the man who'd hired him. Lacy, was an old-time outlaw, one of those you never showed your backside. What Bra-

120

zelton hadn't told him was of how Brock Lacy figured in this, or why Lacy had showed up, but that Gavin Brazelton was worried had been nakedly evident. A lot going on here, the gunfighter mused.

"But I've a hunch it'll be me and Lacy squarin' off."

Tracking the cattle buyer through the red light district, which was centered around Galena Street, had left hard case Red Kiely open to a lot of temptation. Especially when he trailed after Jake Targhee going into Venus Alley. Here the whores sat in languid poses in brightly lighted windows exposing a lot of flesh. Each woman of the line had her own crib, a narrow boxlike room decorated in bold colors. Ahead of him the cattle buyer scooted into one of the cribs.

But the hard case wasn't alone as a steady stream of men clogged the alleyway, old and young alike. There was a ribaldry of noise coming from the alley and nearby streets. Kiely sidled around when he heard the shriek of a police whistle, but it was farther up the alley. Mingling with the miners were a few Chinamen, as everyone sought these bodies for sale.

"Selling their souls," commented Red Kiely, though he saw a few women in the cribs he wouldn't turn away, and not all white women either but mulattoes, Japanese, Chinese.

Stationing himself by a light pole, the hard case was in the midst of rolling a smoke when he sighted in on Brock Lacy turning into the alley. Since Kiely was one of the few there sporting a cowboy hat, He didn't bother with a wave. Then he said to Lacy and the others coming up, this time with a sort of wave toward one of the cribs,

"He's in there."

"Good enough. Me and Kiely'll handle this. You two keep looking for that Texan and . . . the other one, Collier. You find either one, beeline to the Comique."

"We can take them out," insisted one of the hard cases with a sneer.

"Like you took the Texan out at that cafe over to Billings. No gunplay until me and Kiely are there to make sure the job's done right. Awright, take off."

Waiting until their companions were moving away, Red Kiely said quietly, "You're awful damned hard on them, Brock . . ."

"Nothing's holdin' them hereabouts, Red. But I reckon they'll stick now that we're flush again."

"Lookin' at all these whores, Brocks, reminds me of that cowgirl . . . you know, up there in the mountains. She had guts killing herself like that. Me, I'd find an easier way to commit suicide."

In a grouchy aside Brock Lacy said, "She just might have lived through it. Until I learn otherwise to me that woman's still alive, can be a witness against us, too." He took a careful look about as from a nearby street came the clanging of a patrol wagon. Warily he nodded to Kiely. The pair of them began weaving through the passersby. The weapon Brock Lacy figured he would use was his Elliott palm gun packing four .32-caliber slugs. In that crib he was closing on his Colt's would sound like a cannon, and as for taking the cattle buyer out with a knife—the outlaw didn't want to come out of there with blood on his clothing. He pitched the way it would be to Red Kiely, who muttered,

"Take out the woman, too?" Hesitation danced across his face, then he added, "Yeah you're right about leaving her behind to finger us." Behind the narrow panes of the window the garish red curtain had been drawn, and the hard case brought his hand to the door latch, jiggled it, scowled. "It's locked." He turned to face Lacy in the narrowness of Venus Alley, with the night shadows lifted aside by the presence of street lamps and light pouring out of crib windows.

Lacy brushed by Red Kiely and simply threw his shoulder against the door to have it spring open. He hurried into the crib to view a scene he'd seen many times before, the couple entwined on the bed, and—

The bed occupying one corner, a stove in another, a coal hod and bundle of kindling nearby. A small dresser with a wash basin, and on the unpainted walls a few art pictures, one of a pastoral scene, and photographs of some unclad women and one of a man Lacy assumed was the whore's pimp-of-the-moment. Prickling the air was an assorted stench of disinfectant, hair oil and cheap perfume. Gaping in shocked surprise at the intruders, with Kiely closing the door, were the cattle buyer and the black-haired whore.

"Make one sound," warned Brock Lacy, "and both of you are dead." He took a step in closer, and then Lacy slugged the woman alongside the jawbone, and she fell over Jake Targhee sprawled naked on the bed.

"Please, my money's in my coat . . ."

"Shut the hell up." Brock Lacy didn't waste any time as he slapped the butt of the gun at the cattle buyer's hairline, then as Targhee went limp he grabbed one of the pillows. He held the pillow over Targhee's face, brought the gun in to sink it into the pillow and pulled the trigger. The leaden slug passed into Jake Targhee's mouth and got lodged someplace in the back of his skull, and he was dead when the outlaw pulled the pillow away.

"Hardly heard the damned gun go off, Brock," Kiely said nervously as he kept glancing at the closed door, and back to what his partner was doing.

The woman went the same way, with a bullet from Brock Lacy's gun punching into the front of her head. But she groaned as she died, and with her arms flailing about of their own accord as of a puppet doing a jig. Shoving past Kiely, Brock Lacy fingered the curtain aside.

"Seems okay," he mumbled after a while. Kiely found the cattle buyer's coat, and discarded it once he'd pulled out the wallet.

Then the hard cases eased out into the alley and headed to the west, one of them still shaken by what had happened, but Brock Lacy not giving a damn as he had two others to kill.

Chapter Nine

Behind in the cloudy haze of afternoon lay another place of bitterness, of diminishing terror for Reba Jo Cade. Only when they had made a stop at Silesia, did Reba Jo get out of the stagecoach and look back to lift her troubled eyes to the distant Absaroka range.

They were the eyes of a woman changed forever by tragedy. The face, her whole bearing, was of a woman suffering from within. Clad in a simple gingham dress, and with a cloak and veiled hat, Reba Jo whispered a silent thank you to those who'd found her coming down out of that terrible pass gorging upward into the mountain. That she'd survived at all sometimes seemed too difficult to comprehend. "Shad, to be so young . . . and have this happen . . ." It was while making her way down along the gorging of the mountain stream that Reba Jo had come across Shad Jarrett's broken body. All she could do was to drag the body into a rocky cairn, and then press on.

Those who found Reba Jo brought her down into the settlement of Roscoe. The clothes she wore, the money she carried, were farewell gifts to the woman they'd saved. While recuperating there, she was told of it being a stopping place for outlaws heading to rocky hideouts in the mountains. So instead of burdening these people with the tale of how she came to be up there, and perhaps endanger their lives, Reba Jo buried within all that had happened.

Less'n half a day later the stagecoach brought its passenger toward the outskirts of Billings, its night lights shimmering below long slabs of rimrock. One of the first things Reba Jo had done upon arriving at Roscoe was to pen a letter down to Texas. If Guy Jarrett was still there by now he should have received the letter.

"But knowing Guy, he would have headed up this way . . ."

"Stage station's just ahead," called out the driver.

To Reba Jo, after being cooped up in such a small place as Roscoe, the town they were entering seemed to be almost too large. But here in Billings she hoped to find out about the cattle they had brought up from Texas. Or hope against hope that someone else had lived to tell of what happened down along the Crow Indian reservation. The stage pulling up told her they were at the station, a big building on a wide stretch of downtown street. One of the passengers, a bewhiskered man with a friendly smile, got out first to bring back a helping hand. And then with the one valise in hand, Reba Jo Cade headed away to find a hotel.

Not all that far from the stagecoach office the brick facade of the Pioneer Hotel drew her into the lobby. She acquired a second-floor room facing onto the thoroughfare below. As Reba Jo set about unpacking her few belongings, she took stock of her present situation. First of all, there wasn't enough money for the long journey back to Texas. Though her first priority would be to write Guy another letter to give her present address.

"Guy . . . alone with all those señoritas . . ." By now he must have given her up for dead. A person can only grieve so long. Though it was different for Reba Jo Cade. You let go after a while when someone died of natural causes. Branded forever in her mind, she felt, would be the horror of what happened. Branded so vividly, especially in her dreams at night, were the faces of those killers. The names tripwiring through her dreams . . . Brock Lacy . . . Thatch . . . the one called Benson . . . the cattle buyer, Falcone.

"Those . . . bastards . . ."

She brought a hand cupping to brush wayward hair away from the side of her face, felt her eyes misting, though Reba Jo had cried herself out a long time ago. Now the hunger pangs told her she'd missed supper, and listlessly she strode to one of the narrow windows and stared out at the downtown street. Around nine o'clock, she reckoned, an hour when respectable women kept to their homes. Her glance came back along the street to a saloon opposite blaring out honky-tonk music. A sign in a window told of a free lunch being served to its customers. Saloons weren't new to Reba Jo, as back home that was about all small cowtowns had as a place to socialize.

"Well, if I want some of that free lunch I'll have to partake of a drink . . . maybe a glass of beer . . ."

When Reba Jo reached the street, she held on the sidewalk as a couple of dogs scampered by, and a man and a woman jogging their horses upstreet. A light wind ruffled at her skirts as she crossed over, went past four horses hitched out in front of the saloon. Pushing through the batwings, she simply moved over to one of the vacant tables and sat down. Her presence brought the gaming action to a halt, and the music, then everything picked up again.

There weren't any barmaids but just a lonely bartender, who hesitated before easing out from behind the bar and coming over. "Evening, ma'am?"

"Evening yourself. I'm staying across the street at the Pioneer Hotel. Came in on the Red Lodge stage. Your sign out front does say you serve a free lunch; but I'd be happy to pay for it . . ."

"No, no," he stammered, "free lunch, yup, its spread out on that back table. But . . . I shore can fill you a plate . . . and . . . and . . ."

"A glass of beer."

"Glass of beer? Yeah, yup, guess you're old enough, ma'am."

"Hey, bardog," came a raucous voice, "I'm buyin' that pretty filly anything she wants."

Nervously the bartender wiped his hands on the apron tied around his waist, then Reba Jo said, "I can handle it." She took in a rangy cattleman scraping his chair away from a table. He tramped over in an uncertain gait, and Reba Jo knew he was carrying a load of whiskey; the stench of it also told her that.

"Hate to see a pretty filly sit by her lonesome, so reckon I'll join you." He reached for one of the chairs.

Calmly, and with a sweet smile gracing her face, Reba Jo said, "Why don't you crawl back into your hole."

128

It didn't register at first, then the cattleman's face got all ugly and twisted up, and he reached to wrap a big hand around her arm, "No damned . . ."

"Murdock! Ease away from her . . . now . . ."

The cattleman swung sideways and glared at a man just rising from a table, the man holding some cards, and with a badge pinned to his vest. "None of your business, Sheriff."

Sheriff Mason Taylor decided it was, as he slapped down his cards to begin threading around the tables. "Anybody can tell the lady's no streetwalker, Murdock. And why do you want to mess with her anyway seeing's as how you've already got a wife and a batch of younkers. That's it, go back to your buddies." He grinned at the cattleman sulking away.

"Thank you . . . Sheriff . . ."

Tipping his hat back, Sheriff Taylor said, "You're new in town. Don't see many pretty as you around either. Me, I'm Mason to my friends — Sheriff Mason Taylor." He sat down easily and had this puzzled glint in his eyes as he did so, then he asked, "Expect you're out of Texas?"

"Yes, my home. Or was. I . . . my name's Reba Jo Cade."

"Reba . . . Jo . . ." All of a sudden his eyes got all squinty, and he sort of stiffened in the chair.

"Yes . . . is there something wrong?"

In a disbelieving whisper of a voice he asked, "Would it be Reba Jo Cade—?" But he knew the answer even as Reba Jo spoke her last name. "Then . . . then for damned certain all of it's true . . . what Jarrett told me . . ."

"Guy, was he here?"

"Here and gone, ma'am."

"Where, where did he go? I've got to know!"

"Ma'am," he replied while glancing around, "Reba Jo, I reckon we'd best keep our voices down. Your Guy Jarrett took off for Butte; back a few weeks. He . . . he . . . tried piecing together what happened. I expect to you and the rest of them. But you . . . ma'am, you were there . . ."

Uncertainly the bartender held out the plate of food, and at a nod from the sheriff, he put the plate down before Reba Jo and a glass of beer. She smiled her thanks, unable for the moment to find any words. But that Guy had been here spoke of his love for her and concern for everyone else. "Please, Sheriff, I, I hate to drink alone."

"A glass of beer then. Take your time, ma'am, as I'm still about as shook up over this as you are. You know, you're the last person I expected to see. Then to have you drop in here . . ."

"Guy, how did he look?"

"I guess thinned out as he'd been doing a lot of riding. Spoke of you a lot, ma'am . . . and of, of other things . . ."

"Sheriff, about all I have left is the memory of what happened."

"A terrible burden to carry around. By the way, his brother, Guy Jarrett's brother, is still alive. Crow Indians found him. According to Jarrett though, his brother's mind is all twisted out of sorts."

"Wayland, alive, I guess I needed to hear that. To hear that someone had survived."

"I reckon, Miss Cade, you're the only witness to what happened out there. Which means your life could be in danger."

"Then you must know who's behind this," she said candidly.

"Brock Lacy's gang did the actual killings. They were hired by . . ."

". . . the Divide Cattle Company. What else do you have?"

"A name is all, Miss Cade. That being Deal Falcone. One thing, and you might not like this, but I'm gonna have some of my deputy sheriffs keep an eye on you. Being the only witness to what happened is gonna get out sooner or later. You must understand that as sheriff I'll need your statement on this: names, where it happened, and so on."

"Yes, you'll have that. But whatever I say, sheriff, can never bring back . . . my father, the others . . ."

The testimony of Reba Jo Cade brought further indictments against the outlaw Brock Lacy and his henchmen. The only thing is, the outlaws had disappeared, as it seemed had everyone else connected with the Divide Cattle Company.

Reba Jo's hotel bill and other living expenses had been picked up by the county clerk's office. While for her it had been hours of pouring out the tale of murder to both the federal judge assigned to Billings and other law officers. She'd grown weary of it, and too, having those deputy sheriffs stumble around after her.

One spark of hope had been a letter sent by Guy Jarrett to Sheriff Taylor, who'd shown the letter to Reba Jo. She took note of the return address on the envelope, had in fact dispatched a letter of her own to Butte. But a letter wasn't enough, not nearly enough after all she'd been through, the love she

131

had for Guy Jarrett was an agonizing pain in her heart.

It was a Wednesday morning, it was still hazy down by the broad expanse of floodplain of the Yellowstone River, it was time, Reba Jo'd decided, to head for Butte. And when she left her hotel it was through the back door, to go from there to the railroad depot. Her train pulled out around ten o'clock.

But it wasn't until a quarter of noon that a cleaning maid came down to tell that the woman in room 212 was gone. One of the deputy sheriffs, having just come into the lobby, hurried to bring word of this to Sheriff Mason Taylor.

"Sooner or later I figured this would happen."

"What do we do, Sheriff, head out after her?"

"What we do is hope and pray she finds Guy Jarrett. Could be he's pulled out of Butte, as my letter to Jarrett came back. As for now, all I can do is get word to the police over there."

Sheriff Mason Taylor left the rest unspoken. He'd decided after listening to Reba Jo Cade's testimony that whoever was behind these killings was in Butte. That's where Brock Lacy has headed, that cattle buyer, and now Reba Jo.

He told his deputy to watch the office, then Sheriff Taylor put on his hat and left to make tracks for the telegraph office. "She's in danger, Reba Jo. Just hope these killers don't catch her before she finds Guy Jarrett. Be a terrible thing to happen."

Chapter Ten

In his room at the Florence Hotel, a tired Guy Jarrett finished drying his hair, the upward movement of his left arm causing a pain spasm. Other muscles ached, and using a shovel the last four days had put blisters on the palms of his hands. Being a miner, he'd decided, was one tough job. But it was Saturday night, payday, and the prospect of making the rounds with Muggy Callahan and other new friends brought him dropping the towel on the bed and picking up a new plaid shirt.

When they gathered, it was down in the spacious lobby of the hotel. One of the miners gestured at the copy of the *Evening Intermountain* he was holding, "How about these two murders over on Venus Alley. A whore . . . and . . . a cattle buyer named Targhee . . ."

"May I see that?" asked Guy Jarrett. The article was on the lower portion of the front page, but sure enough it was one of the cattle buyers he had met.

"Somethin' wrong, Guy?"

"Don't rightly know," he replied. The police, the article went on to say, considered it a robbery. The night of the murder Jake Targhee had been seen flashing a roll of money in a string of saloons. He left the newspaper there, headed outside and got into a hack waiting at the curbing.

The transom hack started out on it's way to Skibereen's One Mile Limit Ranch, a bistro located east of the city. Guy Jarrett was a troubled man. The police had it wrong as Targhee's death had been cold-blooded murder: the woman killed because she'd seen the killer. Both of them would still be alive had he not come to Butte. But he had no other choice, as this was where that killing cattle buyer had headed. All of a sudden Guy felt washed out, the feeling in him like a blind man getting suckered into a game of high-card stud. Because what cards had been dealt him? Other than a name, Deal Falcone. Something has to break, was his forlorn thought. Muggy Callahan nudged Guy's elbow.

"Here, have a swig of this, Texas. Cause you look awful darned low."

"Obliged." He raised the bottle of Three Star Hennessy to his mouth, found that it was top-shelf brandy, passed it back. Going barhopping had lost its flavor, as Guy's notions were to find the owner of that cattle company, the one Jake Targhee had worked for. But he held to the hack, to let the outskirts of the mining camp fall behind.

After getting his first glimpse of Columbia Gardens set amidst a lot of trees, Guy could see beyond in a canyon lofting up the mountainside the roof of a large barnlike building encircled by a high fence. Spearing through pine trees against mossy rocks were the last vestiges of sunlight, and higher up glistened a few patches of snow. Passing huge screening boulders, there were a few carriages and horses tied outside the fence, and more inside. A flick of a coin, and it was one of the miners paying off the cabbie, with Callahan drawing Guy aside as their cronies trooped into the main building.

"Me friend, you've told me damned little of why you're here. But I sense a deeper motive than just a job . . ."

"Reckon there is, Muggy. But it seems all I've been chasing is a ghost."

"That story in the newspaper, about this Targhee. As I recall Targhee was one'a them cattle buyers. You being a cowboy . . . well, Guy, I won't pry into your affairs. Just hope you catch this ghost before it catches you." A big easy grin loped across Callahan's face as he clapped Guy on the back. "Skibereen's awaits us."

"Bigger'n I expected."

"There's a tunnel back of here with a natural spring runnin' through. Best damned drinkin' water around. If its water you're craving."

Entering, they found a dance in progress out on the large floor and a lot of rustic furniture scattered about the cavernous room. The crude bar where Callahan brought Guy Jarrett was carved from rough pine slabs, and it was long and lined with drinkers. White-shirted bartenders were hard-pressed to keep up with the demands for whiskey and beer and more exotic liquors. Under huge roof logs across the dance floor a band of five was playing some sort of Irish song. Surveying this, a drink was shoved into Guy's hand.

"Here's to Skibereen, a true Irish son."

The seven miners and Guy raised their glasses to toast the owner of the road ranch. One of them nudged Callahan and muttered, "There's some of them damned Cousin Jacks; don't they know they give the place a bad name."

135

"Easy, Fitzsimmons. Leave them buggers be. Look about at all the loose women. Ah, there's one pleasing to me eyes." Callahan strolled toward the scattering of tables, and the others followed to leave Guy by his lonesome by the bar and nursing his drink.

With the music cutting away, the dancers flocked back to their tables or headed for the bar to replenish their drinks. And Guy stepped over by a support beam, lifted his left hand and smiled at the calluses forming over blistered skin. This would hinder his handling of a gun, but first he had to find that elusive Deal Falcone. From Callahan and through a lot of bar talk he was beginning to piece together the makeup of the Copper City. One thing about Butte, he'd learned, that it wasn't outsiders starting the bar brawls but those considered denizens of this mining camp. Miners from around the world had flooded in, these men generally banding together with their own race, the Irish, Serbs, Finlanders, and a host of others. There was the union, which Guy joined or he would have lost his job at the Neversweat. And he felt comfortable, though he was about the only one here, decked out in his old spurred boots and western clothing. Callahan and most here wore box-backed coats, high-heeled shoes, and high-roller hats. The women had on expensive gowns as it was boom time in Butte.

The band broke into a waltz of sorts, while Guy, emptying his glass, was about to turn away from the dance floor. Out onto the floor came a woman enticingly clad in a shimmering light green gown. It seemed as everything became blocked out for Guy except the necklace the woman wore, its green and pink hues matching the abalone tints of Guy's ring.

Abalone pearl necklaces weren't all that common, especially one in the shape of a heart. He found himself stepping out onto the dance floor, as Guy Jarrett had to know if certain names had been etched into the back of that heart-shaped locket. He moved to intercept the woman and her partner.

"Hey, Joey, this gent wants to cut in." The woman didn't seemed to be all that displeased as she had a wide smile for Guy.

"You're making a mistake," snarled Joey Brazelton.

"Ma'am, that necklace, where did you get it?"

"Why, my boyfriend here gave it to me."

Brazelton shoved at Guy's shoulder and said through ugly eyes, "I did, as if that's any of your business."

Guy could tell the man was drunk and spoiling for a fight, but he held there as he said, "Mister, it'll be my business if certain names are etched on the back of that locket . . ."

"Yeah," the woman pouted, "come to think about it, there's some names on my locket. So what, mister?"

"Would one of them be Reba Jo?"

"Why, yes. Joey, just who is this Reba Jo?"

Somehow Joey Brazelton knew the necklace was connected with that business of Gavin's over in Billings. The necklace didn't mean a damned thing to him, and he was finding out that despite her charms the whore was a demanding woman. Under their accusing eyes Joey's anger got the better of him, but at the moment he didn't know quite what to do, other than walk his woman off the floor to get away from all of this. Then when the stranger asked that he be given the necklace, Joey Brazelton

137

lost it. Spitting out angry curses, he dipped a hand inside his coat toward his shoulder holster.

The gun was just clearing leather when Guy grabbed Brazelton's arm. Guy carried a hideout gun, but he didn't want gunplay—he wanted this man alive. They struggled for possession of the gun clutched in Joey Brazelton's hand, and Guy sensed the other was weakening, then it happened. A surprised look flickered in Joey's eyes as his gun fired, and he suddenly went limp in Guy's arms. While around them everyone had stopped to watch the encounter, Joey Brazelton's woman eased away into the press of dancers.

Lowering Brazelton to the floor, Guy realized the man was dead, and then someone cried out, "He killed Joey!"

"For no reason at all."

"Get the police in here."

"You, mister, hold it right there . . ."

Wild-eyed, Guy Jarrett looked about for the woman. It was going all wrong, the accidental shooting of Brazelton, his woman taking off. The necklace; without that he didn't have any evidence to what happened to Reba Jo Cade. The necklace had both of their names etched on it, as did the ring encircling one of Guy's fingers. The necklace was all he had left of the woman he loved, and now he bolted toward the bar and along it, knowing he had to get out of there. To be arrested would see him being charged with the murder of Joey Brazelton—as he was the friendless outsider. He barged outside just in time to see a carriage pulling away.

"Too late," he muttered bitterly. Then Guy had to duck in behind some shrubbery when out of the road ranch came men looking for him.

138

But Guy Jarrett wasn't without friends, for one of them moved to intercept the flight of the woman wearing the abalone pearl necklace. Muggy Callahan caught up with the woman just short of one of the exit doors, and he grabbed her arm.

"Easy," he said around a quick smile. "I want me friend's necklace. Give me that and you can leave."

She struggled against his grip and spat out, "No, it's mine, you damned thief."

"Any damned Brazelton is a thief," he countered. "And all you are is a two-bit whore as that's all Joey Brazelton ever takes out. Sorry about this." He ripped the necklace away from her neck and thrust her away. "Go before I hold you for the police."

Instead of rejoining the others he'd come with, Muggy Callahan went outside in the hopes of finding the Texan. He knew that the report of Joey Brazelton's untimely death would be carried to his brothers. Then the Brazeltons would send their pack of thugs and gunmen in search of Guy Jarrett. By now, he surmised, the Texan would be heading back into town and perhaps to the Florence Hotel to gather up his gear. Callahan got into one of the transom hacks idling out in the big inner yard.

"Back to town, me bucko."

"Sure, and just what the hell is going on in there?"

"A minor altercation is all." He pulled out the necklace and held it up to have moonlight filtering in through the open window set it to shining. On the back of the locket, as he'd overheard back in the road ranch, was indeed the name of a woman. "Reba Jo? No sense plumbing the mystery of who she is. Just hope Guy shows up back at the hotel."

* * *

The bedsprings creaking brought Guy into a wary crouch as he reached for his hideout gun. And then Muggy Callahan said, "A long walk in from Skibereen's."

Only now did Guy Jarrett realize he was framed in the lighted doorway. Crossing the threshold, he closed the door and put his gun on the dresser, along with his hat. He got a lamp going as Callahan swung his legs down and sat up on the bed. "Here, you might want this."

"The . . . necklace?"

He reached out a tentative hand to take the necklace. Guy turned it over and read the inscription on the back of the locket, allowed bits of sorrow to come into his eyes. "About all I have left . . ."

"Left of what, Mr. Jarrett? There seems to be a lot going on here."

"Nothing that I want you to get involved in, Muggy."

"But this Irish son is involved. Took that necklace from Brazelton's woman. You killin' him was accidental, Guy. Me and the others will testify to that, as well as most everyone who was out there. That ring you're sporting, matches the necklace?"

"Yup, bought them down in Old Mexico some time back," he said pensively. In him now that he was holding the necklace was the sure and bitter knowledge that Reba Jo was dead. "Belonged to the woman I planned to marry. But . . . she's dead . . . same as the others . . ."

From the folds of his coat Muggy Callahan extracted a bottle of whiskey. He uncorked the bottle and handed it to the man sharing this small bedroom in the Florence Hotel. And he said firmly,

"Cutting out of here is, I expect, part of your im-

140

mediate plans. Guess I would, too, now that the other Brazeltons will be hunting for you."

"This . . . Joey . . ."

"One of three brothers. Look, Texas, we've shared a lot of drinks and the dangers of the mine . . . and our friendship. If I'm to help you, Mr. Guy Jarrett, your opening up might help."

"This necklace," Guy began, "is part of a bloody story that carries clear down to Texas. Cattle are involved and a lot of killings. You still want to hear it?"

"I gather you plan to stick around?"

"Have to now, I reckon."

"But not in them cowboy clothes," Callahan said sagely, and as he drank from the bottle. "Ah, a savoring bit of the spirits always helps. Mining, Texas, keep working at the mine as what better disguise could you have around this old girl of a mining town. As for Muggy Callahan, I've got a lot of friends in town owe me certain favors. I'll tell you more about those high rollers the Brazeltons afterward . . ."

Easing onto a chair, Guy Jarrett shrugged his indecisions away. He would try to involve Callahan as little as possible in what was to come. But he needed to know more about these Brazeltons, and too, Callahan's friendship.

"Reckon it all started back in Texas . . ."

141

Chapter Eleven

No sooner had Reba Jo Cade arrived in Butte than she was headed uptown in a covered hackney. Arriving before her had been a telegram sent by the Yellowstone County sheriff to Butte's chief of police. Reba Jo didn't know of another hack trailing behind hers, nor did she care, as the only thing on her mind right now was finding Guy Jarrett's hotel.

It was hot, in the low nineties, the open windows of the moving train offered some relief from the heat. But here in Butte jutting to either side on a barren hillside the heat was oppressive. She wanted to do something with her hair before she saw Guy, and her clothes clung to her willowy body, but even the thought of these things were held in check by Reba Jo.

"A year is a long time not to see the man you love."

She let this occupy her thoughts, the fact he could have fallen out of love with her. But, no, not her Guy, a man shy around women but ever so courtly. Should she unload her grief on him? By now he knew what had happened to the others. "No, for now it is enough that they have each other. Later, perhaps, when all of this is over."

There really was an Overland Hotel, with the driver of the hack not bothering to help out his only passenger. She paid the driver, turned eagerly to face the hotel wedged in along the busy street. Suddenly she was nervous, and not at all sure just what to say to the man she loved. Hesitant steps brought Reba Jo into the lobby, small and boxy and covered with old yellowed wallpaper, the man behind the desk the only other occupant.

"A room?" His voice came out kind of whistling between the gaps in his upper teeth.

"No, please, Mr. Jarrett's room . . ."

"Jarrett . . . humph . . ." He spun the register book around to thumb through the top pages.

"Guy Jarrett's from Texas . . . a, a rancher . . ."

"Nope, got no ranchers checked in here."

"But he's got to be here. He, he wrote that he was staying here, here at the Overland Hotel."

"Lady, I'm just the day clerk. There's the night clerk, or there's our manager. And here's the register; goin' back to a couple of months ago. See, no Jarrett's in the book."

Barely able to control her fear and her anger, Reba Jo Cade moved away to find the open doorway. She didn't go outside but held there, fighting the nausea churning in her stomach, confused and uncertain as to what to do next. Should she go back and accuse the desk clerk of lying? Or, if she had one, hold a gun to his head to get at the truth of Guy Jarrett's whereabouts?

"He's lying . . . lying . . ."

What was it daddy always said, mused Reba Jo as she went outside to venture downstreet, *to put on your poker face when things got tough.* Right now she had to do more than that, the least of which was to steel her heart to the possibility of Guy being dead. And don't cloud your mind with womanish emotions, for she felt so strongly that he was still alive, someplace nearby, and in search of those mindless killers.

"Yes, our illustrious sheriff over at Billings," murmured Reba Jo, upon coming to an intersection to shield her eyes from the noon sun. "That I was the only witness to my father and everyone else getting killed. Well, I reckon if that fall into those rapids didn't do in this Texas gal, these hombres over here won't either."

"Excuse me, ma'am."

In turning that way Reba Jo saw the flash of the man's badge, and two more men seated in the covered buggy which hadn't been there a moment ago. "I'm Detective Elkington, Miss Cade. Please, will you accompany us to police headquarters—"

Accepting at face value that the man was really a detective, Reba Jo moved over to crouch into the back seat of the buggy. Then they were clattering away, and with her wedged in beside one of the detectives and with her valise between them. "I guess the sheriff over at Billings was concerned about my welfare after all."

"That he was, Miss Cade," said Elkington from the front seat. "Other people from Texas have written to us requesting answers we haven't been able to give."

"You mean other herds were stolen besides ours?"

"Seems that way, Miss Cade," the detective said as the buggy was brought around behind the main police station.

And in a few minutes Reba Jo was led into the

office of Chief Jere Murphy, and he came around his desk to shake her hand. "Sorry you didn't find Guy Jarrett, Miss Cade."

"You've seen Guy?"

"All we have is some correspondence from Billings, from the sheriff over there. Please, sit down. Elkington, bring us some coffee. To put it mildly, Miss Cade, you've been through hell."

"It hasn't been easy," she agreed, her eyes still asking questions about Guy Jarrett.

Chief Murphy moved back to his chair and sat down, to say, "This town is busting at the seams, spreading out past the flats and edging closer to Anaconda every day. They come from all over, Miss Cade, to work in the copper mines. A tough life. As for Jarrett, he didn't leave any forwarding address, as you've found out. Okay, here's what we have." He had a smile for Detective Elkington who placed a cup of coffee on his desk after a cup had been handed to Reba Jo.

Murphy went on, "The other day a cattle buyer was killed. At first we figured it was just another robbery. But whoever did it took out the woman, too. Some woman working out of Venus Alley, if you get my drift. This Jake Targhee worked for a cattle company headquartered down by the Northern Pacific's main line. Gainsforth owns the company, and Gainsforth claimed your Mr. Jarrett had dropped in some time before."

"At least somebody's talked to Guy. What did this Gainsforth tell Guy?"

"Very little, as Gainsforth had been laid up a lot last year. Left Targhee and a man named Buzz Collier run the operation. So now Collier has disappeared."

"Whoever is behind this is covering his tracks."

Dumping the contents of a manila folder on his desk, Chief Murphy said, "This is the statement you gave to the people over at Billings. Quite a story, to be truthful about it — That cattle buyer, Falcone, showing up out there with some drovers . . . you Texans heading out to this road ranch with Falcone . . . the ambush. Then you, Miss Cade, being taken up into the mountains. And, your desperate attempt to get away by jumping your horse over that cliff. Yes, it's quite the story."

"You do believe me?"

"Oh, Miss Cade, indeed I do. The stolen cattle were only the beginning . . ."

"I don't understand — "

"Butte was in dire need of beef after those bad winters of two years ago or so. What with the population swelled to over fifty thousand . . . and they don't grow crops or beef here, Miss Cade, but dig for copper. So those behind these killings reached down into Texas. Your people and others responded in a way that got them killed." He lifted the lid from a bowl on his desk. "Oh, sorry, try sugar to sweeten this sour coffee. There you go. So, as I was saying, there's more to this dire plot than cattle. Someone made a lot of money selling cattle as prices had skyrocketed."

"Someone from here, Chief Murphy?"

"What we figure, me and Elkington and my other detectives. It would serve these people no good just to let this money lay fallow. So what's here but the mines and smelters, which takes a lot of money to own. Trying to follow a money trail, Miss Cade, isn't easy. Either these people have invested in some working mines or have gotten into the game them-

146

selves. We're working on this. Which brings us back to a certain Reba Jo Cade."

"What I know of this?"

"As far as we know you're the only living witness."

"Guess I don't like the sound of that," murmured Reba Jo.

"Not only does this cattle buyer want you out of the way, Miss Cade, but so does the outlaw Brock Lacy. From what I've heard Lacy has headed this way. It could have been Lacy killing that cattle buyer and the woman. In any case, perchance we catch this Deal Falcone. What it comes down to is your word against his. As the cattle are long gone, and one twenty-dollar bill looks the same as another."

"Wait!" Reba Jo brought a hand up to her neck. "That cattle buyer; he took my necklace. The one that Guy gave to me. Guy had it made down in Old Mexico . . . and a ring that he wears."

Detective Elkington opened a note pad. "Please, could you describe this necklace . . ."

"Yes, yes, it was so pretty . . . made of abalone pearl . . . green and pinkish. My name and Guy's were engraved on the back of the necklace." She inhaled deeply, and blinked away the beginnings of a tear.

"Abalone pearl necklaces aren't all that common to these parts. So, Elkington, check with the local jewelers in case they might have some in stock. Then have your men check out the pawn shops."

"Seems to me," frowned the detective, "a report came in not all that long ago . . . something about a necklace. Or maybe it's nothing, Chief."

"Look into it just the same. As you for, Miss

147

Cade, alive you can help us put these men behind bars. Really, I don't mean to alarm you . . . but we can't afford to have you roaming the streets by your lonesome. We've got to keep you under constant watch, which means Elkington and his men."

"What about Guy? I must find him. He must know that I'm here, that I'm still alive."

"I wouldn't put it past these men that they know Mr. Guy Jarrett is here. That someone was watching the Overland Hotel. Or it could be one of the desk clerks has tipped them off that a beautiful young lass from Texas was in the hotel asking about Jarrett. "So" — he shrugged with his hands — "it means putting up with the Butte police for a while."

"Chief, if it means catching these . . . these monsters, anything is worth it."

"Don't fret none about that, Miss Cade, something'll break in our favor."

"And there's Guy . . ."

"Out there someplace, in harm's way, I'm afraid. It just could be though, that Jarrett is closing in on the people behind these killings. Just hope and pray he doesn't get killed in the meanwhile."

Chapter Twelve

It had been destined to happen, lamented Gavin Brazelton. A sad ending to the dismal life led by his brother, Joey. He stood alone in the cemetery, the few mourners including his other brother had departed. He kicked at a clump of fresh earth and muttered offhandedly, "So long, Joey. The damnfool would still be alive if he hadn't stolen that necklace."

Pieced together by Gavin Brazelton was just what had happened out at Skibereen's road ranch. The luck of the draw that cowboy being out there to spot that whore bedecked with the necklace. But at least the rancher's daughter he'd taken the necklace from was dead. He hadn't told Mako any of this. But there was one thing puzzling Gavin Brazelton, the news about a woman showing up at the Overland Hotel to ask for Guy Jarrett. Then the police had picked her up.

"You sure she asked about the cowboy?" Brazelton asked one of the men sharing the back of the carriage as the driver set it into motion.

"What that clerk told me, Gavin. She had a Texas twang to her voice, so the clerk said."

"That fool clerk wouldn't know a twang from a

mouth organ." That he was worried showed in the pondering set to Brazelton's wide face. He wasn't a man who believed in the supernatural, his notions being that things happened in their natural order. You were born, raised hell, died. But the description passed on by the hotel clerk was uncannily close to that of the woman owning the abalone pearl necklace. Only he had Brock Lacy's word as to that cowgirl being killed up in the Absarokas. Should have let her keep the damned thing, Gavin raged inwardly. As his taking it had led to Joey being done in.

He lashed out, "Just where in hell is that meddling Texan anyway?"

The pair seated facing the man they worked for had separate jobs — Kincaid, the big, double-jowled man in the rumpled brown suit, headed up a gang of local thugs; Waverly hung around to keep trouble from Gavin Brazelton and was more of a messenger boy. He had red blotches marking his rubbery face, and a drooping lower lip. He said, "That woman, she could lead us to the cowboy."

"Got a lot of people looking for Jarrett," Kincaid said defensively. "We'll find him."

"The police, we've got to find out where they're hidin' that woman . . ."

"It's dawned on me, Gavin, that just maybe . . ."

"Just maybe what," retorted Brazelton as he snapped at the driver to pull over.

"This Texan, Jarrett, doesn't know this woman showed up."

"Yeah, that's somethin' to chew over. Okay, Kincaid, this is where you get out. I want somethin' out of the money I'm paying you and your bullyboy." Gavin Brazelton slammed the carriage door to just miss the departing Kincaid's coattail. "You can find me at the Comique."

Usually he could keep his emotions under control, but there'd been too many unsettling events in the last few days. His carriage continued up Broadway. Gavin pushed aside the recent memory of his brother's pine box being lowered into the ground and thoughts of Guy Jarrett and the mysterious woman the police had in their custody, he assumed. As he figured it wouldn't be too much longer before Kincaid's men would stumble upon the Texan.

The carriage pulled into the alley behind the Comique, Waverly got out to hold the door open for Gavin Brazelton as a light spattering of rain hit down. Turning in the open doorway to look back, Gavin said, "That whore of Joey's, the one he gave the necklace to, wait until later tonight then kill her." It was a decision of impulse, but it served to take the edge off Gavin Brazelton's grouchy mood. He sidled around to head inside, as he didn't deem it necessary to explain his reasons to a hired hand such as Waverly. But he figured he had reasons enough, in that his brother Joey could have told the whore too much.

"Joey hadn't been himself lately, moody as hell at times, bragging around town about things better left unsaid. Anyway, she might have a plot next to Joey's; then he can blab to her through all eternity for all I give a damn."

There was another Brazelton deciding to keep secret certain matters from his brothers. Mako had always been fond of Joey, but he shared Gavin's opinion that their younger brother had become a liability. First of all, there was Mako's not revealing to Gavin that he'd been about to have their new gunfighter, J. D. Valentine, gun down their brother. Secondly was of Mako Brazelton's caching a lion's share of the profits derived from their mining and smelter operations in Chicago banks. With Con McLean running things over at the Tenderloin Mine, a tunnel had been dug into land claimed by the nearby Neversweat, and there, as Mako had promised, was a rich vein of the red metal, the pilfered ore being processed in his smelter, a lot of the money also winding up in Chicago.

It pleased Mako Brazelton that one of the political parties had invited him to a dinner party scheduled for tomorrow night. Word was getting around about the brash newcomer, Brazelton, and Mako had absorbed enough local lore to know that if one wanted to survive here in Butte one had to become involved in politics. It wasn't so much that he had any intentions of running for some office, but that he could use his money to elect those favorable to his future plans.

"Best move I ever made was coming to Montana."

Lazily he stretched his arms over his head, with a glance out an office window revealing long shadows jutting away from smelter smokestacks. Farther away sunlight still struck upon the hillside city of Butte, but he welcomed the coming of night. As tonight would see the demise of the outlaw Brock Lacy. He hadn't especially liked the way Lacy had taken out that cattle buyer, felt there'd been no need for Lacy to kill that prostitute. Luckily for him and Lacy the police report listed it as a simple robbery. You'd think Brock Lacy's men could keep quiet about the killings, or about them taking out the other cattle buyer. He would have let Gavin handle this, but the chief job requirement here was a man had to be fast with a gun in order to have a chance against Lacy.

"J. D. Valentine didn't seem too disturbed when I asked him to do it. Even when I told him there'd be a bonus he takes out the rest of Lacy's men."

He rose from behind his desk and was turning to close the wall safe when his secretary appeared. "Mr. Brazelton, some men want to see you."

"Not now," he scowled. "Tell them to come back tomorrow morning."

"They're police detectives, Mr. Brazelton . . ." At his wondering nod she stepped aside to have Detective Elkington enter the office and with another detective close the door but station himself by it.

"Well, gentlemen, how can I help you?"

"Mr. Brazelton, I'm Detective Elkington." Removing his hat, he brushed his thick brown hair back. "Kind of hot out there. Ah, this concerns your brother, Joey, ah . . ."

"Joey? Joey's dead. Buried my brother this morning. And now this . . ." That he resented their presence was evident as Mako Brazelton went about the business of closing the safe door and spinning the dial. Now, turning to face Elkington, he added sarcastically, "Does Chief Murphy know you've come over here?"

"Just doing our job, sir, an investigation we're working on." He removed from his coat pocket a small picture, held it up to reveal that it was of a necklace spread out on velvety cloth. "This picture," Elkington lied, "was taken some time ago. What we have here is an abalone pearl necklace that was

153

stolen along with some other jewelry. Seems your brother Joey's girlfriend was wearing it the night he was killed."

Mako laughed, as he had expected something other than this, and he said, "Perhaps, Joey picked it up in some pawn shop. He was always giving his girls things, necklaces, and what have you."

"You have never seen this necklace before?"

"Nope," Mako said candidly.

Detective Elkington had dealt with these matters long enough to know when a man was telling the truth; and this puzzled him. Quickly he sorted out what Reba Jo Cade had told him about the necklace. While her description of Deal Falcone, the bogus cattle buyer, certainly didn't come close to matching Mako Brazelton. "Tell me . . ."

"I've told you all I know. A necklace?" Mako laughed again as he shook his head. "One that Joey gave to a whore. Maybe it wasn't Joey but this whore stealing the necklace—"

"No, Mr. Brazelton, since the necklace wasn't stolen here in Butte but elsewhere. The necklace belonged to a woman named Reba Jo Cade; a rancher's daughter. Out of Texas, I might add. The man doing the actual thievery of the necklace called himself Deal Falcone. This Falcone stole a lot of cattle, too, Mr. Brazelton, cattle that were driven up from Texas and headed for Butte. The cattle got here all right . . . but the Texans owning them and their men were left for dead back east of here."

Deliberately, Detective Elkington had come in there with a smoking gun. Over the past few weeks, even before the arrival of Reba Jo Cade, he'd been aware of the Brazeltons. Of how these brothers seemed to have suddenly come up with a lot of

154

money, then to have Mako Brazelton buy into mining property. There was Joey, nothing but a two-bit punk, but always seeming to be flushed with money. And the other one, this Gavin Brazelton, whom he'd finally tracked down as to hanging out at the Comique. His next stop after leaving there was to go over and brace Gavin.

"I'm sorry, Mr. Brazelton, that your brother is dead. But it would clear up a lot of things if we knew just how Joey came into possession of this necklace. You still insist you haven't seen this necklace before?"

"No, dammit, I haven't," blazed out Mako.

"Again, my condolences." Elkington and the other detective let themselves out of the office and the building, and got into their buggy. He didn't say anything until they had pulled out of the smelter grounds and were on a wide thoroughfare. "Pull over here."

"Sure," the other detective said quietly. "You really got Brazelton's goat. "The Comique; are we still going there?"

"We won't be the only ones, I'm figuring."

"You really laid it out in there."

"Had me a smoking gun for sure. Look, about all we've got is Reba Jo Cade . . . and . . . and just this hunch of mine about Mako Brazelton. He doesn't match the description of Reba Jo's cattle buyer. But there's his brother, Gavin."

"And here comes the other one, Mr. Mako Brazelton. Wonder how much a fancy carriage like that costs?"

"More than what we make. Easy now, let him get up the street a piece. As to why I told Brazelton so much, well, it just might help us smoke out that

Texan, too, Guy Jarrett. He's a lucky man having a woman like Reba Jo Cade."

"Only he doesn't know she's alive or even here in Butte."

"Yeah, but for how long?" The worry of this accompanied Detective Elkington up the bustling street. He was playing more than a hunch, as he felt about as strongly as a man could that things were about to break wide open. Part of his worries concerned the arrival in town of this outlaw gang of Brock Lacy's. While word had been brought to Elkington by one of his informants of still another gunfighter drifting in.

"Hired guns . . . a grim business."

"They still behind us?"

"Still hanging in there." responded Kiki Brown as he brought the bay into a trot. Back a few blocks the mine whistles had sounded to announce the end of the working day for miners, and a lot of these men were trudging onto the sidewalks in search of saloons. The driver of Mako Brazelton's carriage saw his chance to elude the buggy following behind, in the form of an ore wagon blocking the street ahead. A back wheel had broken under the weight of the load the wagon carried and some ore had spilled out onto the street. A draught beer wagon was coming downstreet. A touch of his whip and the bay broke into a faster gait, with Kiki Brown bringing his carriage past the debris on the street, then he reined sharply to the right and was into an alleyway just as the beer wagon was moving to block the buggy from pursuing.

"Nice work, Kiki." Mako took in the back doorway of a saloon, and he told his driver to slow down as he braced to swing down. "Keep tooling this rig around town."

Mako jumped down and claimed the recessed doorway. From here he watched his carriage pick up speed, then a few moments later the detectives surged past in their buggy. "Bastards," he muttered vehemently.

He was more than disturbed at the grilling he'd received from Detective Elkington, as he couldn't believe that his brother could do something so stupid as to latch onto that necklace. "Sell us out for a cheap trinket! Dammit, Gavin, this isn't the Barbary Coast."

His anger was under better control as the Comique loomed up spilling out light and ricocheting noise though the sun had barely gone down. He took the back entrance and the steps with a fluid upward stride, where one of the barmaids pointed out the gallery box occupied by Gavin Brazelton. A mine owner known to Mako chose that moment to come out of another box, the man's polite nod taking him toward the back staircase. Lighting a cigar, Mako strode on, set smile on his lips.

"Mako?"

He stared down at his brother seated alone in the gallery box, and Mako closed the door before he eased down at the table. "Today's been a bad day."

"Yeah, too bad about Joey."

"Just the two of us now," Mako said casually as he watched his brother empty the glass of whiskey. He was calmer now, thinking on one hand here was his brother, weighing all that he'd acquired, all that property and the money. Maybe it was that Gavin just acted in character when he took that necklace, but still he had to square things, and Mako said coldly,

"The law just left my office. Seems a certain necklace turned up in town. The one that caused Joey to be killed . . . the one you just had to have . . ."

Gavin Brazelton's eyes lidded over and he stiffened in the chair. He knew that when Mako decided to do something, it was quick, and to the point, and now under the table Gavin's hand eased to the gun tucked into his waistband.

"But we can't change what happened. Joey—anyway, he was becoming a liability." Mako reached up to push his hat back, a smile unfrosting his eyes. "First this damned Texas cowboy shows up . . . and now some woman looking for him . . ."

"Got a lot of men out looking for the cowboy." Gavin Brazelton grimaced, as it was becoming damned clear to him that Brock Lacy hadn't killed that cowgirl after all. "Ain't it about time we did something about Lacy?"

"Part of why I'm here. As tonight it'll be that gunfighter I hired bracing Brock Lacy. Guess, though, I should have had Lacy taken out before. The other problem is yours, Gavin. You find that cowgirl."

"Now where the hell am I supposed to look?"

"What happened out there that she's still alive?" countered Mako Brazelton.

"It was Lacy's men," protested Gavin, "promising to kill her after they'd had their way."

"No matter. The point is, her testimony can see you hanged . . . see what we've worked for ruined. I don't care if they don't sleep for the next month, Gavin, but get these thugs of yours out scouring the

158

streets for her. The coppers, they've got her hid away. She's the only one asides Lacy that can finger us."

"I'll tend to it," scowled Gavin Brazelton as he braced to shove up from the table.

"After you find her bring her to me . . . out to the smelter. But alive, you hear. I want to know what she told the coppers before we kill her." Mako Brazelton left first, went out the back door and afterward kept to sidestreets and to a saloon where he expected the showdown to take place between Brock Lacy and the gunfighter. If perchance Lacy got lucky and downed J. D. Valentine, Mako would be there to backshoot the outlaw.

"Can't leave nothin' to chance anymore," he groused. "With Lacy dead . . . the cowgirl's next . . . an' then that meddlin' Texan . . ."

Chapter Thirteen

Tracking down the woman who'd been with Joey Brazelton had kept Guy Jarrett away from his job at the mine. So far he'd come up empty-handed, the fear in Guy the woman could have left Butte. Purposely, too, had Guy kept away from the Florence Hotel, as he didn't want to get Muggy Callahan or others he called friends involved in something that could see them get killed.

Still stamped in Guy's mind was the dark but jaded beauty of the woman. She had sort of amber-colored eyes, flecked with a cold indifference, and musing it over again, Guy had the feeling she'd been playing Brazelton for a fool. One thing had Guy's search for her revealed, that there were a lot of seedy cathouses and saloons tucked amongst the many sections of the city. Another, that it was hard getting anything out of these closemouthed people, as the clothing Guy wore was that of a rundown miner.

He still got shivers over what took place last night. His search for the woman had taken Guy Jarrett out to a Meaderville saloon. Nothing had come of it, however, and he'd left. Then he'd been jumped by a pair of cutthroats. With the whacking of a knife into a dark wall just about head level, Guy had reacted quickly, decisively, by throwing himself off the boardwalk and out into the street. He came up just as quickly with his gun palmed. They hadn't expected this, the pair of ambushers, but when one made a move to throw his knife, Guy's revolver belched hot flame. As he'd intended, the bullet punched into the man's knife arm, with the other one breaking away, and Guy had let him go as he closed in on the man clutching at his arm.

"Don't shoot . . . dammit . . . you busted my arm . . ."

"Next time, scum, I'll geld you. This wasn't just a mugging . . ."

"We . . . figured you for an easy mark."

"No, there's more!"

The dry crackling of the hammer being drawn back by Jarrett caused the wounded man to yell out, "The Texan . . . you're the Texan they're after . . ."

"Spill the rest."

"I, all I know the word's out. A hunnard bucks to the man findin' the Texan."

"You knew Joey Brazelton—"

"Damn, I'm bleedin' bad . . ."

"I could go for your other arm."

"Yeah, Joey, a real bad one, yeah?"

"That woman of his, you knew her?"

"Hell, Brazelton had all kinds of women . . ."

"The dark-haired one, kind of pretty, was wearing a necklace the night Brazelton was killed."

"Got to be . . . that bitch, Sybil. Worked over at the Alley Cat . . . over on Silver Street."

That had been last night, and Guy knew the word of that encounter would have been carried back to

161

the Brazeltons. He'd learned that one of them was a miner owner, the other brother matching the description of cattle buyer Deal Falcone. By rights all of the mining property owned by the Brazeltons was his, and Reba Jo's, Wayland's, belonged to a heap of others.

But all he had linking the Brazeltons to the killings of his friends was the necklace he'd given to Reba Jo. His ring and the necklace he packed in a money belt snugged around his waist, and a few greenbacks. Sometimes he felt the ghost of Reba Jo Cade was alongside walking these dark streets, maybe the whisper of her voice urging him on.

Once a starpacker, Guy knew he had to have hard evidence before going to the local law. This woman of Joey Brazelton's, this Sybil, had every right to hate him for what he'd done. Joey, a braggard among other things, must have told her some interesting things. "So they, Joey's brothers, would get to her sooner or later, as they'd taken out those cattle buyers.

On the dark end of Silver Street a few blocks removed from the glittering lights of downtown Butte he came upon the Alley Cat saloon. One lonely red light hovered out front, the windows covered with black paint, Guy reckoned to conceal the sins of what went on inside. There'd been whitewash on the board walls, flakes of it still there. Just inside the open front door toward which Guy stepped there was an inner entryway and another door through which he shouldered. Heading out of the saloon, and with Guy having to sidestep, was a big, hardeyed man clad in a rumpled suit. Briefly their eyes locked, the man's eyes sliding away as he figured Guy to be just another miner.

162

Over creaking floorboards Guy moved toward a table occupied by four women, two of them smoking hand-rolleds. One of them fluffed up her hair as Guy came up. "Howdy, sport; I'm Daisy."

Spewing out a ring of cigarette smoke, another asked, "You lookin' to have some fun?"

Guy returned her smile as he glanced about, then back at the woman who'd spoken. Does Sybil still work here?"

"Why . . . ?"

The one called Daisy cut in, "Not no more."

"Someone was just in asking about . . ."

"Dammit, May, shutup. Now, sport, just why are you looking for Sybil . . . ?"

He fingered a silver dollar out of his pocket and set it down on the table, and he said quietly, "Reckon she's kind of special, if you get my drift."

"Mister, a dollar won't even buy you a bottle in here."

"Expect not." Two more dollars were set down by Guy. "I keep this up, won't have enough to have a go with Sybil. She here or not?"

"Upstreet a couple of blocks; second house on the left, or she could have moved out . . . as she hasn't been here the last couple of days."

"Someone else was asking about her?"

"Gent that just left. You don't find Sybil, come back."

In the next block, Guy found houses that were crammed together, two-story affairs with entrances for those living on the ground floor in front. A few people were enjoying the evening air from front porches, and a dog came out to growl as Guy passed by. But his concern was that someone else was looking for Sybil.

"Gent back there," he mused, "had a certain look."

He passed the first house in the next block, with the narrowest of gaps between it and the house where he expected to find the woman, Sybil. No lights showed on the ground floor, the vaguest of light came through an upper window. Then he heard the sound of breakage followed by a muffled scream, and quickly Guy cut in through the gap between the houses. A protruding nailhead clutched out at his coat sleeve to rip it just before he came out into the back alleyway. Here he found stairways leading up to covered porches and laundry hanging from clotheslines, and to the fear of Guy Jarrett, the shattering of window glass jerked his eyes upward.

It seemed to escape from her assailant, the woman had thrown herself through the closed window. She hit the upper porch floor hard and cried out in fear and pain, and now the man Guy had seen in the saloon yanked the back door open and came out, the barrel of his gun sweeping to cover the woman trying to get to her feet, and again Sybil cried out,

"Please . . . no, please, don't kill me . . ."

The man had one hand pressed against his face and blood seeped through his fingers, and he snarled angrily, "You dirty bitch, you die—" Now he became aware of Guy pounding up the staircase, saw the glint of metal from the gun Guy held, swung to fire, but too late as Guy's six-gun punched out two slugs that reverberated as one. Now Guy swiveled out of the way as down the staircase toppled the ambusher, falling limply and dead.

Sprinting up onto the porch, Guy went to the woman, who gazed back at him out of eyes filled with panic and the fear of what had just happened. Guy said, "Easy, Sybil, I'm a friend. Easy, now." His work-hardened hand reached out to steady the woman, with her reacting like a filly about to be broke to the halter, sort of skittish, and with a purpled bruise on the left side of her face, and her black raveny hair maned out wildly. The sleeve of her dress had been torn, and it had a low neckline to reveal to Guy a lot of creamy flesh. Just for a moment he wondered how a woman as pretty as this could become someone of the demimonde. But whore she was, and had known Joey Brazelton.

"He . . . he broke in." Now, just like that, a puzzled gleam came into her eyes, the dawning of recognition, and she blurted out, "You . . . killed Joey . . ."

"Didn't mean to, Sybil. He was all liquored up . . . and it just happened. Did Joey give you that necklace?"

"Yeah, he did. But someone took it from me. Just . . . just who are you?"

"From Texas. An' the necklace, Sybil, it belonged to the woman I was to marry. Are you okay?"

"Come," she finally said, "people are coming out. Come inside . . . please."

And as Guy did so, he knew that someone would call the police, that his staying any length of time could see him arrested. He looked about at the wreckage caused by Sybil in her attempt to get away from her assailant, and he said,

"The man who tried to kill you was sent by Joey's brothers. I'm afraid they want you out of the way."

"But . . . why, all I did was go out with Joey."

"Their fear is what Joey could have told you about their operation here."

"Yes, he did talk a lot, about a lot of things, I guess. I've got to get out of here, out of Butte. Texas . . . you're from there? Joey did talk about some . . . cattle, I believe, something his brother Gavin was mixed up in."

"Those cattle are why I'm here."

"You mentioned a woman . . . the one the necklace belongs to."

"I'm afraid, Sybil, they killed her along with others I knew. Drove the herd on to Billings. From there the trail led here. These are heartless men, brutal men, none meaner. And that's saying a lot as I was a Texan Ranger once. Sybil, please understand, I need your help, as all I've got for evidence is that necklace Joey gave to you."

"What can I do?"

"Tell what you know'll be enough."

"Please, mister, I . . ."

"I'm Guy Jarrett. And begging you to help me. They're after me too, Sybil. Between us we can put these murdering Brazeltons behind bars."

"Someone's coming up the stairs," she warned Guy.

"Any other way out of here?"

"No, just through the back door."

"You can stay here and take your chance with the law, or . . ."

The apartment was small, the kitchen and two other rooms, and she followed him out of the kitchen into the living room saying, "No, I, I'll let them in, stay here."

Opening a front window, Guy turned to face her, and he said, "Tell them my name. And about Joey,

166

but it's up to you, Sybil." He flicked a glance kitchenward when someone began rattling the back door panes. "But . . . whatever you do, Sybil, consider that you wore the necklace belonging to the woman I loved. Reba Jo was her name, and both of us need your help. Consider that."

Crouching out the window onto the roof of the front porch, Guy lowered himself over the side wall, then dropped in the gap between the houses. He'd cleared the houses and was striding away when a hand clamped onto his arm.

"Don't try it!" warned a burly policeman; and then Guy was aware of other uniformed police closing in. He brushed his coat open, to have one of them take his six-gun. Next came handcuffs steeling around his wrists, something he used to do to outlaws, the feel of them a sobering reminder that it would be the testimony of Sybil which could either clear his name or see him sent to prison.

"Now what would a simple miner be doing with a weapon such as this?" came a policeman's Irish brogue.

"Down in Texas I used it on varmints."

"Texas is a long ways from here, me bucko. Bring up the paddy wagon now, boys. Murder; you want to tell us just why you killed that man? Make it easier on you."

"Guess that would take most of the next hour or two."

"Well, they can listen to your story down at the station house. Into the paddy wagon now."

Chapter Fourteen

It wasn't too long after the Texan was lodged in a cell that one of the turnkeys slipped away and headed for a tavern on Silver Street. He arrived there to find Reed Kincaid and some of his street thugs about to pull out.

"He's charged with murder, Mr. Kincaid."

"Here, Dugan, for your troubles."

He dismissed the turnkey with an impatient smile. From here he would relay the news of Guy Jarrett's arrest to the Brazeltons. But there was more, for at last he'd discovered where the police were hiding the woman. Kincaid was too wily a man just to rush in with blazing weapons. So to this end he'd had his men keeping watch over the house down where the flats meandered toward Silver Bow Creek.

"There's a change of watch at midnight," he told the thugs clustered around his table, whiskey spillage and a deck of worn cards on it, and Reed Kincaid's rimfire .31-caliber Cone. "Four keep watch; sharpshooters, I figure. A couple more inside with this Reba Jo Cade."

"Rifles — been a long time since we've used them."

"Only way," snapped Kincaid, "we can take out those badgepackin' bastards."

"See no reason for keepin' that cowgirl alive . . ."

"What Mako Brazelton wants. Half past eleven, so let's head down there."

The fringed carriage driven by Kiki Brown seemed to have traversed every downtown street before it was sighted by those following it veering away onto an eastward road. In the trailing buggy, Detective Kirk Elkington said with a trace of irritance,

"What kind of game is Brazelton playing?"

"Yeah, he must be wise to us tailing him."

Elkington pulled his watch out of a vest pocket and peered at its face, and he said worriedly, "Guess it has been a waste of time. After eleven. What about . . ."

"Mr. Brazelton giving us the slip." He flicked the reins to pick up the pace of his horse. Small pebbles kicked out from under the wheels as he brought his buggy alongside the carriage. He veered in closer forcing the carriage closer to the ditch, and shouted, "Pull up or it'll be the ditch for you."

Barely had both vehicles come to a stop than Elkington was hopping out. He yanked a carriage door open, knew as he'd suspected all along that Mako Brazelton had used him for a fool. Slamming the door shut, he glared up at the man driving the carriage. "By rights I should lock you up."

"On what charge?"

"Don't push your luck. Tell Brazelton I'll be hounding his heels. Now head out." He stepped back as the carriage lurched into motion, and then Elkington got back into the buggy. "Why would Brazelton pull such a prank? Unless . . . unless . . ."

"The Cade woman?"

"Has to be it." And even as Elkington spoke the other detective was U-turning the buggy around on the dark stretch of road, and then with his reins lashing out to jolt their horse into a gallop.

The days of being confined to this two-story clapboard had worn heavily on Reba Jo Cade. Sometimes in the cool of evening she'd been allowed to go for a walk, but hemmed in by detectives commanded by Kirk Elkington. She'd chafed about all of the reasons the police had given her for not arresting Gavin Brazelton and his brother. Evidence being too flimsy, that just Reba Jo's testimony wouldn't be enough to convict a man as clever as Mako Brazelton. There were other reasons having to do with the laws out here.

"But those who killed my people used the law of the gun."

Reba Jo Cade's damning words were stopped by the windowpane of her upstairs bedroom. "Evidence; something crafted by lawyers . . . and judges. Seems my testimony just isn't enough."

If only, and every time she thought about the abalone pearl necklace given to her by Guy Jarrett a sadness enveloped her, the necklace could be found. Had not that murdering cattle buyer ripped it from around her neck on that killing night out there. How could she ever forget the face of that man, with the image she'd had of him given to the police. A flamboyant dresser, a big man—certainly someone of this description shouldn't be all that hard to find.

As for Detective Kirk Elkington, certainly competent, but perhaps too unyielding when it came to bending the law. Elkington's explanation that he was building a case that would stand up in court would be laughed at down in the Lone Star state. There the two adversaries more often settled any matter in a gun duel.

Finally, there was an embittered Reba Jo Cade. Even if these killing scum were found, what then? Scattered by predators out on the plains of Montana were the remains of those she'd loved. Their deaths must be avenged, but listening to the idle chatter of the detectives keeping guard over her told a lukewarm story of how justice was administered in the courts of this copper city. A story of clever lawyers and in some cases crooked judges, of how criminals could buy their way to a lighter sentence.

"From what I hear, these Brazeltons have a lot of money. And connections. The police . . . they've been helpful. But in the end, I reckon . . . it'll just be this Texas cowgirl and the man I love . . ."

She turned away to check her appearance in the dresser mirror, the eyes gazing back at her seemingly that of an older woman. Every day she would steel herself to the fact that when Detective Elkington put in an appearance, it would be to tell her that Guy Jarret had been killed. Here Guy was, scouring the streets of Butte in search of the killers, and unaware, she was absolutely certain, that she was alive. Why hadn't Guy gone to the police? Even more implausible was that the police hadn't found one lonely Texan.

"Guy, dammit, I know you're still alive. So . . . darling, take care."

The steps of Reba Jo carried her to the open bedroom door and out toward the staircase. The first few days here had seen the meals prepared by different detectives, and somewhat badly. Then she'd simply taken over the kitchen, a routine of preparing meals that helped to give her mind some peace, keep her thoughts away from so many worries. So her presence at this late hour, as noted by the pair of detectives loitering in the living room, was merely routine. The coffee she'd already made. Reba Jo put on the table sliced pieces of cheese and sausage, then went over to pick up a knife and slice out hunks of apple pie.

She called out gaily, "Coffee and pie if you guys want some." Then she went to the back door and eased out onto the back porch, where her smile took in the man seated on the back steps, and his companion idling by a picket fence. "Made some apple pie . . . and there's cheese and sausage."

"Ma'am, you're a real gem. You know my wife says I'm packing on more around the middle."

"I could bring it out?"

"Nope, we'll take turns in the kitchen." The man rose from the back steps to follow Reba Jo into the kitchen, and she held there for a while, chatting with men she'd come to know even as her eyes went to the wall clock; a quarter of an hour short of midnight."

The change of watch was punctual, she'd learned. And what Reba Jo Cade had in mind must be accomplished before then, with her apologetic words that she was going to bed bringing her out of the kitchen and upward.

In her bedroom, she bypassed the two windows opening onto the front of the house and went to the only side window. The window was opened silently by Reba Jo, though the nervous expelling of air

172

from her lungs seemed to tom-tom out against the wall of the next house, one of many wedged in thick along this southern stretch of city street. To her now came the voices of mining machinery, thick-throated and vibrating, with the stench caused by the smelters floating into her room. Just like that a cat let go with a piercing scream to give her momentary pause, then another cutting loose told her of two toms fighting over territorial rights. Stealing to the closet, she swung the door open and reached down for the sheets she'd tied together. She dropped them on her bed, reached back for the light summer coat and the handbag heavied by the weight of a revolver.

Her plan to leave was haphazard, contrived out of desperation. Part of it involved searching for Guy Jarrett. The rest of it Reba Jo's hopes to find that bogus cattle buyer. Then—he'd either talk or die.

Shoving a corner of the bed closer to the window, she bent down to tie one end of the sheets to the bed frame. She let the long sheet rope drop out of the open window, held there to stare down at the opening between the houses, and the way the front porch of the next house would become part of her escape route. She donned the coat, and slung the strap of her handbag over her shoulder, and crouched out the window to grasp the rope of sheets. Quickly, she lowered herself down the rough wooden wall, then let go and landed hard.

Gathering herself, Reba Jo waited there in a watchful crouch. Besides the two watching out back, and the two inside the house, at least three more policemen would be out front but hidden amongst deeper shadows cast by other buildings.

Now she went up, to grasp the porch railing of the neighboring house. Lithely, she worked over the railing to drop lightly onto the porch. There was a slight creaking of floorboards, a sudden intake of night air by Reba Jo. Then she scurried across the porch to begin lowering herself down onto the fringe of barren ground.

With one shoed foot groping for the ground, there came an expulsion of the sound as of a shoe scraping over gravel, and Reba Jo Cade was suddenly pinioned from behind, one man wrapping his arms around her, the hand of another clamping over her lower face to cut off her sudden scream.

"Can't believe you'd be so stupid, dearie," snickered one of the men to the woman he held in his arms. As she tried to rip herself out of the man's grasp, he snarled to his companion, "Dammit, use your sap on her."

The booming of a rifle sounded from nearby, and that was the last sound Reba Jo heard as something hard rapped into the back of her head. The man holding her limp body was Reed Kincaid, and angrily he spat out, "No need for that now. Go tell the others we've got what we came for." Then he hoisted Reba Jo over a broad shoulder and hurried back to a waiting carriage.

Detective Kirk Elkington knew there was trouble when he heard the barking of rifles. What he didn't know as their buggy careened around a street corner into the midst of the gun battle was that Reba Jo Cade had been spirited away. The unexpected appearance of the buggy brought an abrupt end to the gun battle, though Elkington did manage to fire

174

back at an elusive shadow fading down an alleyway. He jumped out of the buggy coming to a halt out in front of the clapboard house, his appearance bringing his men moving in close but still looking about warily.

"How'd they find her?"

"In this town there are very few secrets. Anybody hurt?"

Elkington's question was answered by an upstairs window suddenly being thrown open. "She's gone!"

"Gone? Reba Jo?" Elkington broke running for the front porch. He bolted inside and took the steps two at a time, and there in Reba Jo's bedroom he saw the sheet rope being pulled in by one of his detectives.

"Can't believe she was in cahoots with these thugs . . ."

"She wasn't," puzzled Elkington. "She, Reba Jo, wanted to get out of here, as she told me more'n once. Guess she figured things were coming along too slow. Just her bad luck they moved in tonight."

"Now what?"

"We clear out of here. Come on." He led the wait downstairs, brought those in the house out onto the front porch, as around them a few lights were coming on in other houses.

Detective Kirk Elkington went on, "I want all of you to get a few hours sleep. It's a little after twelve. But at five o'clock I want all of you reporting for duty."

"To go looking for Reba Jo—"

"What she knows will see them killing her."

"Them," snapped an angry Detective Elkington, "are the Brazeltons. Just got word late today that they were driven out of San Francisco. What I don't

175

like are these thieves coming into my town. We don't have much to go on other than what Reba Jo told us. But we owe her a heap for all she's gone through. Five o'clock!"

By his orders Detective Elkington was let off at the main police station in the darkness of a night gone bad. Fully he blamed himself for the actions taken by Reba Jo Cade. Perhaps he hadn't been forceful enough in the way he'd handled the case. But it was a case unique to Butte, and to him as a detective.

Inside he went past the curious eyes of the night sergeant and other policemen to slump behind the desk in his bullpen office. His hat he removed to send spinning onto a wooden chair. Lifting his shoes he planted them on his desk and leaned back in his creaking chair, dispirited at the moment, a thousand details of this case tripping down the worried corridors of his mind.

"Trouble is," he said out loud but in a low monotone, "What Reba Jo told me is almost too fanciful to believe. But the more I get into it, the more every word she spoke is the truth. Consider first of all, Mako Brazelton, slick as they come."

Elkington knew about Judge Clancy's secret deal with Brazelton, and a lot more. This involved some of his informants telling of how Mako Brazelton had set about pilfering ore from other mines. With Mako's background as just a damned thief, his money to get into mining had to have come from selling those stolen cattle.

"I swear if harm comes to Reba Jo, I'll get you Mako, damn you, if it costs me my badge."

176

"This might interest you, Elkington."

Blinking away his musings, he looked up at the desk sergeant moving into his office, and he growled, "What perchance might that be . . . ?"

"What you've been looking for—this necklace."

Elkington swung his own and leaned forward to practically tear the necklace out of the sergeant's meaty hand. He knew without question that what he was gazing at was the abalone pearl necklace which belonged to Reba Jo Cade. Finally he groped out with, "Where'd you get it?"

"A miner was arrested tonight charged with murder. Had that necklace in his possession and somethin' else might interest you."

He turned questing eyes up at the sergeant.

"This miner's sure enough got a Texas drawl."

"Jarrett! Dammit, its Guy Jarrett! Where's he being held?"

"Second floor cellblock."

Plunging to his feet, Elkington paused, and said, "Murder? Anyone I know?"

"Could be, Elkington. Killed a two-bit punk name of Waverly. Over a whore named Sybil, according to the arrest report."

"Sybil . . . Sybil? Yes, one of Joey Brazelton's old flames." He stared at the necklace again, a sudden chord of hope flaring to chase away some of his worry. Now he was brushing past the desk sergeant, hurrying back through the emptiness of the bullpen offices to a staircase. A turnkey unlocked a barred door behind which lay the cellblock cloaked in shadows, the turnkey going ahead down the barred cells.

"Cell five," said the turnkey as he unlocked a cell door, and at a nod from the detective he went away.

Standing there, it suddenly came to Detective Kirk Elkington that the man in the cell, the Texan, wasn't aware that Reba Jo Cade was still alive. That Jarrett had come all this way from Texas spoke of how he felt about Reba Jo, and a heap more. He should have asked the turnkey to leave his lantern behind, but the important thing now was to talk to the Texan, and he moved into the cell, only to have the man huddled under the thin and ratty blanket bestir himself.

"Spell it out, mister," Guy Jarrett said coldly, and as he sat up, and as Elkington moved into the vague aura of light filtering in through the cell window.

"I'm . . . I'm a detective, Mr. Jarrett. And you don't know how glad I am to find you . . . find you alive."

Absorbing this, Guy finally spoke. "That so? Just what time is it?"

"Ah, one or so. Time, though," he held out the necklace, "you knew the woman this belongs to is still alive."

It didn't sink in at first to Guy Jarrett. As a man charged with murder he had few options and fewer friends.

"Yes, Reba Jo's alive."

"Alive," Guy said in a trembly voice, and he rose now to have Elkington pass to him the necklace. "Then she's here?"

"In Butte, yes. Been looking for you, Guy Jarrett; but you've been a hard man to find. But . . . there's something else . . ."

Someone used as Guy was to hearing bad news knew it had to be that, and about the woman he loved. He listened, though in him were feelings he'd

178

kept at arm's length ever since leaving Texas, the recital of the detective about just what had occurred tonight. At Elkington's amiable suggestion, they vacated the cellblock and went down to occupy Elkington's office, the desk sergeant fetching in a pot of fresh coffee. Guy learned all of the horrifying facts of Reba Jo's escapades with that outlaw gang. He was told by Elkington the rest of it.

"The Brazeltons have backed themselves up with money and gunhands and a crooked judge. As for you, Mr. Jarrett, you're charged with murder. But I suspect it was something else? As I know this whore, this Sybil, was going with Joey Brazelton."

"She knows too much. So they decided to silence her."

Yawning, Elkington said, "Going on half past four. My men'll be in soon. I'll have Sybil picked up. But in any case, Guy, I'll see to it those murder charges against you are dropped. Now . . . Reba Jo . . . they have her. My fault."

"Sort of my fault, too, Mr. Elkington." Guy rubbed the nape of his neck; a weary gesture. "My fault for not coming to you first. Then I would have known about Reba Jo."

"You said your brother Wayland survived this."

"Barely," responded Guy. "About all I've got left, my brother . . . and Reba Jo."

"What would you suggest I do?"

Rising, Guy Jarrett set the coffee cup aside. "Call in a lot of favors, I reckon. Its been my experience as a Texas Ranger that lawbreakers tend to make mistakes. Mako Brazelton made a big one when he abducted Reba Jo. But this is your baliwick, Mr. Elkington, and I reckon you know all the hiding places. Am I free to go?"

"Yes, but promise you won't take the law into your hands."

A hardness settled onto Guy's face, the stubble of beard giving him a mean appearance, as did his rumpled clothing. At the moment he wasn't about to reveal what he intended doing to Detective Kirk Elkington or anyone else. Though he realized a direct plan of action was the only thing that could save the woman he loved. A plan that meant him going over to the Florence Hotel to reclaim his possibles sack and the six-gun in it.

Quietly he said, "I'm only one man . . . while you've got the whole police force of Butte siding you, Elkington. I'll keep in touch."

When Guy Jarrett had taken his silent departure, Detective Elkington carried thoughts of the Texan back to a washroom. As he laved water over his face and availed himself of a towel, it was clear to the detective that the Guy Jarrett he'd seen tonight was a very dangerous man.

"Could be Jarrett's goin' to smoke out the Brazeltons. Can't blame him none about that. Can't say he'll come out of it alive—or Reba Jo Cade, for that matter."

Chapter Fifteen

One of the barkeeps at the Collar & Elbow knew something was in the wind. Grisbee, his name was, had tended bar in too many places not to see the signs of trouble, and if he didn't need this job so badly he would have walked out. He took a nervous swipe at the bar top as he took in one of the barmaids sucking up to one of a trio of gunhands. Earlier he'd spotted a known thug slip the barmaid and another girl a few greenbacks.

"Both of them sucking up to those hard cases," Grisbee muttered worriedly. "And that back-alley thug . . . seems to me he hangs out with the Brazelton bunch. Trouble, damn it all, and a good three hours until closing time."

Through the worried fretting of the barkeep the gaming action in the Collar & Elbow went on. It was one of Butte's larger saloons though tucked away from the main streets. Railroaders more than miners liked to come in, a fact which also brought in those new to Butte. The roulette wheels were as crooked as they come, the rotgut whiskey watered down, and the bartenders had the reputation of slipping a man a Mickey Finn to get at his poke.

At the table where he was playing poker, Brock

Lacy took in the lanterns hooked to the wagon wheel fixtures dangling from the high ceiling. The outlaw had been winning steadily from his table companions, a sad-eyed merchant, a railroader clad in overalls and a blue cotton shirt, and a gambler. The two others at the table Lacy had figured as riffraff, but they had ready cash, and that was all that mattered. He watched with masked admiration as the gambler's supple hands flicked out pasteboards to the players.

"You ever think about bein' a sawbones . . . ?"

"A pickpocket, maybe."

Brock Lacy let belly laughter rumble out of his mouth as he picked up the five cards dealt to him. He was in an expansive frame of mind. Had every right to be, for he'd found out more about the Brazeltons. And it hadn't surprised him any them heading up a gang of thieves out on the West Coast. Mako with his blue-blood ambitions, he mused scornfully. Yesterday he'd gone over to that smelter to confront Mako Brazelton, and came away empty-handed but Mako said they'd get together at this saloon. Mako would show, of that Brock Lacy was absolutely certain, as he couldn't afford to have his shoddy past revealed.

The three jacks the outlaw found he'd been dealt brought him tossing a blue chip into the pot. "Raise you, gambler, another fifty; an' I'll take one card."

Gunfighter J. D. Valentine had drifted into the Collar & Elbow about a half hour ago. Idling at the bar over a stein of cold beer, he saw to his satisfaction that the man he expected to call out was still in that poker game. Meanwhile Brock Lacy's pair of

182

hard cases were enjoying the company of some bar girls and drinking heavily. The place was crowded, not with the usual run of miners but with a lot of lowlifes, bunco artists and such.

"A refill?"

"Might's well," muttered the gunfighter, even though there was still a lot of beer left in his glass. It hadn't taken him any amount of time to figure out why Mako Brazelton had picked this scummy saloon. Removed from the mainstream bars, and hemmed in by dark streets, it was most certainly a place where these newfound friends of Brazelton's wouldn't congregate.

Another thing J. D. Valentine had pondered over was of Brazelton wanting to be here when the gunfight took place. Maybe it was in the man's blood, his wanting to see someone killed. Could be another reason was that Mako Brazelton wasn't all that sure he had the faster draw.

"Only one way to find out," retorted Valentine as he left his beers behind to thread back through the tables. Closing in on the table where Brock Lacy sat, he took in the stacks of chips heaped before Lacy, let his glance slide from there to the outlaw's watchful eyes. They sized one another up, Lacy the older man and graying, with that cynical mouth; Valentine's opinion that Brock Lacy wasn't all that fast. Killing Lacy would be just another day's work. A sidelong flick of the gunfighter's eyes took in the hard cases, one of them pouring out raucous laughter as he pawed at the woman's white blouse, and both of them about two sheets to the wind. He'd paid a street thug to come in here and have those whores have a go at Lacy's men; a cheap evener of the odds.

"You want in, hombre?"

"You've got a full table."

"We can make room."

He smiled back at the gambler and said, "Yup, reckon I'm just another woolie lookin' to get sheared." He lifted a chair over as the players made room, then the gunfighter sat down between the gambler and the railroader. Producing some paper money, he bought a handful of poker chips even as he felt the appraising eyes of the gambler take in the low-slung gun at the right hip.

"Boise mean anything to you, stranger?"

He could have shrugged that it didn't, but J. D. Valentine wanted the edge his name would give him, and to the gambler he replied, "It could."

"Thought so," grinned the gambler. "Been some time but it was you sure enough, Mr. Valentine. Boys, should have seen how Mr. Valentine took out those two . . . bammity-bam, and they was crumbled in the street."

Brock Lacy lost that disinterested look. "Reckon that would be J. D. Valentine."

The gunfighter nodded carefully, just as his watchful eyes took in Lacy's right hand going down to brush the tail of his coat away from his gunbelt. "Should I know you?"

The retort stung Brock Lacy, caused a snort of disdain to spill out of his mouth along with, "This must be your first trip to Montana." He glared at the gambler. "Deal them pasteboards."

With the presence of the gunfighter the game took on a somber mood. An hour passed, another, J. D. Valentine oftentimes folded winning hands, though once he just had to buck the gambler's full house with a higher one. The railroader, down on his luck, folded, as did the merchant. As for Valentine, he simply ignored the glaring eyes of Brock Lacy, let Lacy win hands that he shouldn't. Then, just short of midnight, showing up near the crowded bar was Mako Brazelton. And just about in time for what the gun fighter had been setting up.

"Gambler," Valentine said out of the blue, "seems to me that Montana cowboy is awful lucky." Now his eyes speared Brock Lacy. "Too damned lucky."

It took a moment for it to sink in, and when it did, Lacy slammed his cards down amongst his stacks of red and blue chips. Like agates seeing light for the first time the eyes of Brock Lacy glittered how he felt back at the gunfighter. And like the other hard cases, Lacy had put down his share of whiskey, though it didn't show all that much. His words came out trembly as a coyote slinking through corn stalks, "Nobody accuses me of cheating, damn you, Valentine!"

"Who said anything about cheating," said Valentine.

"Gents, now . . ."

"Shut the hell up, gambler. This is between me and this so-called gunhand." Lacy had straightened up in his chairs, saw beyond the gunfighter seated across the table Mako Brazelton standing by one of the roulette wheels but looking his way. This wouldn't take long, came a confident thought, then he'd settle things with Mako. Now the other players vacated their chairs, Lacy's pair of hard cases just realizing there might be gunplay. "You want it here or outside, Mister Valentine?"

Rising, as did Lacy, the gunfighter said softly, "The street is as good a place for you to die as

185

here." Then with an unnerving boldness J. D. Valentine simply turned his back on Lacy and began ambling toward the front door. The presence of so many, and of Mako Brazelton, was his assurance that Lacy had to follow him outside. Once he'd brushed through the batwings, others thronged outside but kept to the boardwalk as Valentine stepped out into the street. Halfway across, he swung around and stood there waiting.

While inside the Collar & Elbow, the outlaw Brock Lacy was checking the loads on his .45 Colts. His anger over being called a cheat was a flame of arrogance that he'd kill the sonofabitchin' gunfighter. Even so, he told the two riding with him to back up his play. "Bastard comes in here and breaks up an honest poker game. You pull leather same time as me. Boise; no gunfighter ever worth his salt ever came out of there."

Lacy kicked a chair out of his way, then he glared at Mako Brazelton about to go out front, and he called out, "Mako, about damned time you showed. You bring that money with you?"

"We can talk about it later."

"Now, dammit."

Through a smile Mako patted his coat pocket. "I've got the money. Don't fret none about that, Brock. But this gunfighter out there, this J. D. Valentine, hear he's sneaky fast. You could call this off, Brock."

"With three against one big mouth, like hell. You just be here when this is over or . . ." The anger of the outlaw carried him outside.

It couldn't have gone smoother, chortled Mako Brazelton. He held there by the batwings, taking in J. D. Valentine standing out in the middle of the

186

dark street, the three outlaws swaggering off the boardwalk to spread out. Somewhere in the shadows of the buildings across the street he'd left his brother armed with a Winchester. The odds, he figured, were decidedly in Valentine's corner, though in a gunfight a lucky shot could take out the quicker draw.

"Damn, I wish there was some way to lay down a wager on this." Then a vicious smile touched his lips, for he knew just how this was going to come out. He pushed outside and filtered in amongst those crowding the boardwalk as the gunfighter spoke jestingly.

"Figured you was too yellow to go it alone, Brock Lacy."

"Uh, I never told you my name."

An easy smile graced the passive face of J. D. Valentine, and he stood there in a relaxed manner of someone chatting casually with a friend. "Know that an' a heap more about you, Lacy. That you like little boys for one thing; like to cuddle up with them."

"Damn you to hell!" The words exploded out of the outlaw, and now he went for his sidearm, an awkward stab at his holstered gun. It cleared leather even as he was going down. When he hit the dusty ground he was still alive, had finally let it dawn on him that this was a setup, and again he cried out, "It was . . . was that damned Mako . . ."

The other hard cases didn't fare any better, one actually triggered his gun wildly. They both felt the killing sting of the gunfighter's revolver — both hit about the same place in the chest cavity. They fell, dying as they'd been born, into the dust of their creation.

187

The gunfighter came out of his crouch, with smoke curling out of the barrel of his six-gun. There was still one load in his gun cylinder, but he took the time to reload as he moved in on Brock Lacy writhing where he lay and trying to stem the flow of deep red blood staining his shirt front. Realizing Valentine's intentions, Mako smiled, mouthed these questioning words,

"What the hell is Gavin waiting for—"

Then it happened, Gavin Brazelton fired his rifle from ambush. The heavy, steel-jacketed slug hit the gunfighter squarely in the back and spun him around. Dying, he stood there on weakening legs and still managed to trigger six bullets from his weapon. He was hit from the front as Gavin Brazelton fired again. The impact of the heavy slug drove him backwards where he toppled down a bare yard from Brock Lacy. Everyone still held on the boardwalk, the crackling of the Winchester still ringing in their ears. Finally, someone yelled,

"Its over!"

"All of them, wiped out, Godalmighty . . ."

Now began the surge out toward the dead gunhands. Mako Brazelton stepped into the street, hurrying over to kneel down by Lacy. The man was mumbling something, incoherently, and dying.

Softly Mako muttered as he leaned closer, "I don't like damned blackmailers. You should'a pulled out of here, Lacy. But your kind never learn."

"He still alive?"

Coming erect, Mako Brazelton said quietly, "Just cashed in his chips. Who the hell was he?"

"Supposed to be a famous outlaw name of Brock Lacy."

"Where he's going fame don't mean a damn thing." Mako hurried away.

When Mako Brazelton arrived back at the Comique, he found his brother just coming into the alley back of the saloon from the opposite way, and Gavin had discarded the rifle. Gavin came in closer puffing contentedly on a cigar teethed around a wide grin.

"Damn, Mako, it went just as you said. But that damned Valentine, that draw of his, faster'n anything I've ever seen." Gavin's excitement took him after his brother entering the saloon and going up the back staircase. They were passing along the private boxes lining the upstairs hallway when stepping out of a box came one of the thugs working for Gavin, and Gavin scowled,

"Wha'cha got, Kincaid?"

"That cowgirl."

"Hey, you hear that, Mako, we lucked out again. Well, she still alive?"

"That's what your brother wanted. But I ain't handin' the cowgirl over until you boys fork over a thousand bucks."

"Why, you . . ."

Mako draped a restraining hand on his brother's arm, and then he stepped past Mako to enter one of the private boxes. His smile included both of them. "Come on, sit down, you'll have your money Kincaid. Tell me about it." Easing out his wallet, he removed some greenbacks.

"Took a lot of time finding her, Mr. Brazelton," the thug said to Mako. "I've got her hid out in one of my livery stables. Could have slit her throat, but

189

you said otherwise."

"Here, Kincaid, a thousand, for you; another thousand for your men."

"Gee, Mr. Brazelton, you're a real gent. What about her?"

Mako consulted his watch. "Let's see, in one hour I want her brought down to my smelter—come in the west entrance. But alive, you hear."

Gavin followed the thug out into the hallway, where he ordered a bottle of whiskey from one of the barmaids, then he rejoined his brother gazing at the action below. He removed his hat and wiped the sweat from his receding hairline as he let the tension drain away. "Plugged that bastard gunfighter dead center; felt damn good. That Texan, he's still in jail, meaning we can get word to him we've got his woman."

"What I figure, Gavin." He broke out laughing, reached out to punch Gavin's shoulder. "What a sweet deal tonight turned out to be. Nabbin' that cowgirl was one hell of a bonus. Now everything's nice and tidy, no one left to spill what they know. You sorry you came to Butte?"

"Only sorry we didn't come sooner."

Chapter Sixteen

There was no mistaking him for anything than a waddy from Texas, as Guy Jarrett wore his gunbelt buckled low over his worn Levi's, the spurs on his boots jingling as he brought the horse the back way out of the livery stable.

A day and half a night ago had seen him released from jail. His first stop had been at the Florence Hotel for a change of clothing. He'd felt a lot better with the .44 Colt's strapped to his side, thinking, that if they were looking for a Texan, meaning these scum of the Brazelton's, they'd sure as sin have no trouble finding this one.

But as for Reba Jo Cade, it was as if she'd vanished from the streets of Butte. Guy had even located Gavin Brazelton's hotel, but it seemed Brazelton hadn't been there for a couple of days.

"Sleeping around," Guy muttered bitterly as he climbed into the saddle. He had simply gone in and stolen the horse, as it was a long walk down to the smelter on the flats owned by Mako Brazelton. Going there was just a hunch of Guy's. Meanwhile, he knew, the police were scouring the city for Reba Jo. There were other properties owned by Brazelton, but the smelter was where Mako headquartered.

As he pulled out he couldn't shake the feeling that Reba Jo was still alive. As men the caliber of the Brazeltons had a bullying instinct. Braggadocio about fit the bill, as they were braggards and killing thieves. He figured Mako Brazelton would keep Reba Jo alive, working her over until she broke to tell Mako all she knew. Then, he'll kill her.

It was another cloudless night, lights from the city driving back starlight, and it was beginning to cool down some from the warmth of day. Now Guy left an alley and brought the gelding at a canter onto Montana Street sweeping southward toward the flats pinpricked by lamplight pouring out of house windows. The street was more a wide thoroughfare, the traffic as it closed on eleven o'clock thinning out. The mines on the downsloping hill, had in them miners working the night shift, with the yellowish glow of lights around the gallows frames as viewed by Guy.

Now he refreshed his mind as to what he'd been told about the Brazeltons by Detective Kirk Elkington. Possessed of an explosive temper was Gavin, who he knew now had posed as the cattle buyer. It had been Gavin who'd let those outlaws take Reba Jo. And Gavin had led his friends away from the herd that night to their deaths.

The other brother, Mako, here was the dangerous one. The one setting up this whole killing scheme. It wasn't so much that Mako was a gunhand, but that he'd have plenty of hirelings around, insulated like the lining of a coat by these gunpackers. To get into the smelter shouldn't be that much of a problem, but afterward —

Sensing his tensions, the gelding fought the reins; Guy's soothing words a balm that brought it back into an even gait. Southwesterly, as he'd scouted out this afternoon from a nearby street, smoke belched from the towering brick chimneys of Mako's smelter, and also from lesser chimneys. The smelter was made up of massive tapered roof buildings of a dirty-gray color. Trestles over which the smeltered coppered ore was transported mazed away from the buildings and to dull-gleaming railroad tracks. Other trestles lowered to loading ramps, up which came huge wagons bearing raw ore — the richness which had caused this copper city to come into being. Operated by day, only a sprinkling of lights showed in the buildings spread out for two city blocks alongside the railroad tracks.

Closing in where the spur line swung toward the main right-of-way, Guy walked the gelding over the iron railings, and dismounted under one of the trestles. Overhead sulfuric smoke was an encroaching cloud holding back the glow of stars. Tying up, he watched a door swing open, then two guards emerged and passed along the building. Guy figured there would be others, and he said,

"The way it is. Perhaps . . ." The fear rose that Reba Jo might not be alive, and Guy chased the fearful notion away. Boldly now he walked in under the sheltering legs of the trestle.

Trailing after the Texan when he'd been released from jail were plainclothesmen. For, and though Detective Kirk Elkington hadn't cleared it with Chief Jere Murphy, he felt Jarrett was determined to find Reba Jo Cade. Another reason was that most of his detectives were known to the Butte underworld. The latest report was of Guy Jarrett leaving the Florence Hotel adorned with his gunbelt. Afterward, and in the early shank of the evening, the Texan had simply vanished.

"Could be dead," murmured Elkington upon turning away from where he'd been staring out an office window at the activity on Gold Street.

"How did he know we had men following him?"

"He was a Texas Ranger, remember. Anyway, I reckon the only way they'll stop the Texan is by killing him."

But someone had picked up the wanderings of Guy Jarrett, and fortunately for him one of Elkington's plainclothesmen. A former cowhand himself, Ed Pierson hadn't been all that surprised when the Texan had donned his old range clothing. Then, as had the two others he worked with, Pierson realized they'd lost the Texan in the network of back alleys. Splitting up, they had continued their search. A hunch of Pierson's fetched him down the very same street taken by a solitary horseman.

It was about here the detective wished he was mounted on another horse, but somehow his running gait down the street had given him a clue as to where Guy Jarrett was headed. Coming of Montana Street into a confusion of houses a watchdog had almost got to him, but somehow he'd kicked the dog away and went on. Winded, and with sweat staining his summer clothing, at last he'd come onto the main line of the Union Pacific, crossed beyond that to spur lines weaving away to venture past trestles.

It was here he came across the Texan's horse. He realized that the dark mass of buildings the trestle connected up with was the smelter belonging to Mako Brazelton.

"I wonder . . . Brazelton wouldn't be that stupid . . . bringing that woman here? But that must be it . . . and the Texan's by his lonesome."

194

The detective was torn between going in to find Guy Jarrett or climbing aboard the horse and heading back to report to Elkington. His worried glance took in the movement of men guarding the grounds and buildings, realized that the two of them stood little chance against so many guns. "Hang in there Jarrett as I'll be back with reinforcements." The horse shied when he came around to untie the reins, then the detective was in the saddle and wheeling away.

Back at the main police station, a worried Kirk Elkington was reaching for his hat with plans to go out and assist in the search for Reba Jo Cade only to have a policeman rush in to give sketchy reports of a shooting over at the Collar & Elbow Saloon. He came out of his office as the desk sergeant said,

"Calm down now, Finnegan. You say there were four of them getting shot . . ."

"I heard this shooting goin' on. By the time I got there four of them were stretched out in the street. They were cowhands, sergeant. I recognized one of them as being the man you're looking for, Detective Elkington."

"Jarrett . . . the Texan . . ."

"Nossir, that outlaw we've been lookin' for . . . Brock Lacy. Funny thing, too . . ."

"Go on?" urged Elkington.

"I'd swear that it was Mako Brazelton leaving just as I got there."

"Mako? Come on, we're going back there."

In exactly ten minutes Elkington came in to where people were still milling about in the street before the Collar & Elbow Saloon. A police wagon stood nearby, with uniformed policemen just beginning to remove the bodies. He got out of his buggy and shoved through the crowd.

"Oh, Elkington?"

"You find out what happened?" he asked as he stared down at the dead face of one of the hard cases, then went on to look at the other bodies. To his relief he found that the Texas wasn't among the dead. "Well?"

"This one, from what I found out, took on these three. Then someone took him out from ambush the ambusher was hidden over there. Used a rifle."

"Now, I want you to question everyone here. Find out if anyone can remember seeing Mako Brazelton as being here when it happened." Even as he asked Elkington knew few answers would be forthcoming.

He went over to get back in his buggy, torn between staying there or returning to the police station. Earlier his request to conduct a search over at the smelter had been rebuffed by his superiors. But the question now was why had Mako Brazelton risked exposure by coming here. He reined away sorting out any reasons Mako might have had. That Brock Lacy had worked for the Brazeltons he already knew. But the man with the rifle, the ambusher? It could only be the other brother. Killing their sordid past, which they intended for those out of Texas.

"Damn, Jarrett, you can't do it alone."

But Guy felt very much alone as he came away from the trestle and beelined for a small shed. He ducked in behind the shed when, from a series of three large building to the south, a couple of guards appeared. Unlike the first guards he'd seen, these men carried rifles, and when they swung in between the buildings, Guy took out after them, hurrying down an embankment to come onto level ground

He passed along the lower wall of a four-story building spaced with windows. A few feet short of the corner of the building, he heard the scuffing of footsteps. And Guy ducked in closer to the wall, draped a hand around his single-action Colt's, eased it out of leather.

One of the guards, his rifle tucked over a shoulder and rounding the corner with an ambling gait, whistling softly failed to see the Texan slipping in from behind. But the touch of cold steel to the nape of his neck cut off the whistling pronto. Reaching over, Guy took possession of the rifle. "One word out of you, hombre" though barely audible, Guy Jarrett's voice was filled with menace, "and I'll ventilate your neck."

"Mister . . . I ain't carryin' no big poke . . . but you can take what I've got . . ." The guard found himself being moved in closer to the wall.

"Where's Mako Brazelton's office?"

"The boss? Why . . . ?" The barrel of the gun jabbed harder into his neck followed by the hammer being thumbed back tumbled out more words. "He's . . . Brazelton's here."

"I expect the woman's here, too—"

"Please, mister, I don't know nothin' about no woman. I . . . I just come on duty at sundown."

"I expect you might be tellin' the truth. Mako's office?"

"Straight down this row of buildings. Swung around the corner and its the brick building off to your left. Mister, there's . . . there's a heap more guardin' the smelter. I'd . . ."

Guy brought the rifle barrel slapping down at the man's head, let the man fall in a crumbled heap. Now he took in the rifle, a Henry, and packing seventeen leaden slugs, and he muttered, "What the hell; better'n my single action." Going on at a trot down the row of buildings, it struck him that it was highly unusual so for many guards to be on duty, which affirmed his belief that this was where Mako Brazelton had brought Reba Jo. "A mistake, you murdering son."

The air was rancid with a mingling of stenches, chimney smoke being wafted away by a sudden wind, the eyes of Guy Jarrett darting around guardedly. Rounding the corner of the last building, long and high as the others, he got his first glimpse of where Mako Brazelton could be holed up, the office building a two-story brick affair with a lot of lights showing.

"Count four men idling around the front entrance," he remarked to himself. The office building was separated from the smelter buildings by a large open and barren yard. He couldn't be sure, but it seemed to Guy he could make out some horses tethered along a side wall. "Probably got a carriage house out back."

The main door stood open, light coming down the hallway and outside. His eyes lifted to the light framing second floor windows. That was where Mako Brazelton should be, and Reba Jo, if she was still alive, and now an anxious gleam came into his eyes, the pain of all he'd been through. To him came the chatter of the men clustered by the main door, laughter, the winking of cigarettes as some of them puffed away, and every man jack of them packing weapons.

"She's here for damned sure," Guy murmured, and as he strode out boldly to began angling on a course that would take him across the yard toward the back of the office building. He was still in shadows, but wary, and now the guards turned as if expecting someone to emerge from the building, but Guy held to the same gait. Then he broke stride when Gavin Brazelton came to stand silhouetted in the lighted doorway.

"Okay, its over. We're pulling out."

"You want us to come along, Mr. Brazelton?"

"Naw, that woman ain't worth worryin' about. Check in your rifles and call it a night."

"She is here . . . but is she alive . . . ?" Now Guy Jarrett began bringing up the rifle to sight it in on one of the murdering Brazeltons.

Chapter Seventeen

The remembrance of that first night was a blur to Reba Jo Cade of fear and the cold of being held prisoner in the lower reaches of a large brick building. A pallor of lights managed to filter through a cobwebbed window during the following day. Little scurrying noises could be heard by Reba Jo, as cellar vermin were becoming aware of her presence. Pulsing through the concrete block wall were the sounds of heavy machinery, once in a while a whistle wailed eerily. To tell Reba Jo this building was part of some mine.

Ropes cut cruelly into her wrists and ankles, and secured so tight that she'd given up trying to free herself. Oftentimes she felt lightheaded, out of sorts with all of this, with pain tremors crabbing out from where she'd been hit in the head. And there was some blood caking in her hair and from the ropes cutting into her flesh.

"How stupid I was," she said. "But . . . but what the hell . . . I've been in tighter spots . . ."

Troubling her as evening shadows crept into the basement room was her simply being abandoned down here. No attempt had been made to see how she was faring, or to bring her any water or food

While bolder encroached the cellar dwellers.

She fell asleep, slept well into the early hours of the evening. Then what roused Reba Jo was what seemed to be a powerful light beaming down at her. Groggily she awoke as two men came forward, one to cut the ropes pinioning her legs, the other man lifting Reba Jo, where she stood on trembling legs, would have fallen had not the man been there to steady her. The one holding the lantern said crudely,

"Not bad looking at that. Think we should have a go at her before we take her to Mako . . ."

"Shut the hell up, Larson . . . as you know what happens to those wantin' to buck the boss. Come on, cowgirl, step along now."

Dimly aware of coming onto a flight of steps, Reba Jo said weakly, "Water . . . please . . ."

"Larson, you was supposed to see she was givin' somethin' to drink."

"Got tied up," he said lamely.

"Your half a brain got tied up. Yeah, cowgirl, soon's we get you upstairs . . . now up them steps."

With cold-blooded reasoning Mako Brazelton had kept the cowgirl tied up in a cellar room. He knew, from being locked up in jail out in California during his younker days, just how it could work on a person. The uncertainties of it all built up, and you'd do most anything to get out. It would be especially hard on someone used to the wide open spaces.

While keeping her here any longer would be pushing his luck. So what he had in mind for Reba Jo Cade brought him up lightly from his chair and over to the liquor cabinet, where Con McLean was just pouring brandy into a glass. Slouched on the arm of an overstuffed chair was Gavin Brazelton gazing out a window.

"You're really hitting it hard, Con."

"I suppose I am at that," replied Con McLean. "Should you have had her brought here?"

"You mean why didn't I have her killed outright," said Mako as he helped himself to some whiskey. "Dead she can't tell me what I want to know. Relax . . . I'll have her purring like a kitten in less'n five minutes. She's the last one, Con, the only one connecting me and Gavin to that cattle operation."

"Yes, I guess you've done the right thing."

The plan as concocted by Mako Brazelton was to get what he could out of the Cade woman. Then he and the woman and his brother and McLean would head over to the Tenderloin Mine. From deep within the Tenderloin men supervised by Con McLean had dug a tunnel into the neighboring Neversweat Mine, had pilfered out tons of high-grade copper ore. Considering McLean's report that the pocket of ore was thinning out, Mako had concluded the tunnel must be closed. A charge of dynamite would not only seal off the tunnel but erase any signs of pilfering by the Tenderloin.

Glancing at his mining supervisor, Mako was beginning to have doubts about Con McLean. In his mind at the moment there was a parry and thrust as to just how far he could trust his mining supervisor. Pilfering ore was McLean directing his revenge at the other mine owners. But when he'd told McLean what his intentions were for the woman, there'd been a drawing back, with Mako spelling out to Con McLean not to consider it murder so much as a way of covering their tracks. That once they'd placed the cowgirl in the tunnel and set off the dynamite charge, Reba Jo Cade would only be a painful memory.

"Did you read the evening paper?"

Both of them glanced at McLean.

"About the gunfight over at that saloon. One of them getting killed was that gunhand you hired, Mako."

"Yeah," he said casually, "read about it. Guess he caught, guess J. D. Valentine caught another gent cheating at cards."

"I heard somethin' about it," threw in Gavin Brazelton. "Why'd you bring that up?"

Lowering his glass, Con McLean sensed the growing tension in Mako's office. He had anticipated violence down in a mine because of their pilfering copper ore, and he could shrug something of this nature off, go on to do the same to other mines. But outright murder, as engaged in by these Brazeltons, went against the grain. Perhaps, too, he'd known all along it would come to something like this, that by simply being here he was an accomplice to what was to come.

Quickly, measuredly, he said, "Because his actions could have brought attention to you, Mako. I suspect more that the others wanted to match their speed with a gun against Valentine's."

Considering this, Mako finally said around a smile, "He was fast alright, was J. D. Valentine." The sound of boots filtering into his office, Mako rose to move over and open the office door, where for the first time he laid eyes upon Reba Jo Cade.

He hadn't anticipated that the cowgirl would be so hauntingly beautiful, despite the dishevelment of her clothing and hair. He took in the full body of a woman who by rights should already be dead. He took in her frightened intake of breath, the way her full breasts filled out the white blouse, and he cast her a sudden smile.

"You've led us a helluva chase, cowgirl. Fetch her in here." Mako stood aside.

Forcibally, Reba Jo was brought into the large office. They made her sit down on a hardbacked chair centered between Mako's spacious desk and where Gavin Brazelton stood by the north wall. With her wrists still tied together, Reba Jo watched as the men who'd brought her here were ordered out of the room, then Mako closed the door. She took in Con McLean trying to keep the concern for her out of his eyes, turned her head to find the other occupant of the room was the bogus cattle buyer.

Gathering herself, all of Reba Jo Cade's bitter and damning anger came out as she hissed, "You murdering bastard!"

"Why you damned hussy . . ." Gavin started toward her.

But from around the desk came his brother, Mako's backhanded blow whacking solidly against the side of her head, and she almost fell out of the chair. He grabbed Reba Jo by the hair and pulled her upright, rained two more backhanded blows across her exposed face, and now blood began trickling out of her nose. Somehow she fought back the tears, though a sob of pain fled out of her mouth. In her eyes there was for the barest of moments this dishabille glimmer, but by sure willpower Reba Jo drove the moment of confusion away. And defiantly she gazed back and up at Mako Brazelton, who broke out laughing.

"Damn they breed them tough down in Texas. Con, fill one of those glasses with whiskey. We'll see if this Texas wildcat can hold her liquor." He grabbed Reba Jo as she broke up from the chair. "Give me a hand, Gavin."

"My pleasure," growled Gavin Brazelton as he

204

came over, with his viselike gripping of Reba Jo's shoulders holding her to the chair.

Mako took the glass of whiskey and looked back at Reba Jo. "I expect you made some kind of statement to the police. What you told them, cowgirl, could get you killed."

"I told them exactly what happened."

"Perchance what is that?"

"Your brother was out there when we pulled in with our herd. He lied about everything. But you know all of this."

"What I know is none of your business," retorted Mako as he brought the glass to her lips and cupped his hand around her chin. "Tastes good, don't it. Tell you what, you sign a statement that you was mistaken about my brother being out there and, cowgirl, we'll let you go."

"I'll sign nothing. He was there!"

As he forced her mouth open, Reba Jo felt the whiskey gushing down her throat, and she gasped. Somehow she managed to close her mouth, to have Mako swear out loud, and then he threw the rest of the whiskey at her face. "You're right, cowgirl, we ain't gonna let you get out of this alive. That statement you gave to the police ain't worth the paper its written on if you disappear." Mako went back around his desk and reached to the coatrack for his hat. "You two, go down and tell the others to check in their rifles. Then meet me out back."

"We should take some of the men along . . ."

"I think we can handle one woman, Gavin."

"There's still a chance that damned Texan might show up."

"Let him, dammit." Mako pulled Reba Jo to her feet, and as his brother and Con McLean left his office, he hesitated while taking in her eyes pouring out hatred. That brought out his anger. "You're a looker all right . . . and you sure as hell need some taming. So, cowgirl, when we get over to the Tenderloin I'll show you what a real man is."

"You're scum . . . nothing but gutter scum."

"Come on," he said laughing, and as he grabbed her bound wrists and pulled Reba Jo along with him. "When we get over there we'll sure as hell have us a roll in the gutter. You'll die, cowgirl, knowin' you was had by the best."

A scowling Gavin Brazelton tramped down the staircase trailed by McLean. He hadn't liked the idea of Mako's of keeping the cowgirl alive. As it wasn't Mako that had been out Billings way, but him. Another fretting worry of Gavin's was it was his sworn belief that Texan, Guy Jarrett, would show up here. They'd almost got him a couple of times, but like in pitching horseshoes close wasn't good enough.

"What time is it?" he snapped.

"Forgot to carry my watch."

"Never mind. I'll just be damned glad when we get her out of here. That dynamite charge all set to go?"

"All you need is a match . . . and then clear out of there. What do you think?"

"Don't start sermonizing about it now, dammit," said Gavin. "Once that charge is lit a hundred ton of rock'll wipe out that tunnel and the cowgirl." He went to the open front doors and stopped there, gave orders for the guards clustered there to call it a night greeted with some smiles as they headed away.

Now alongside McLean, he went up the short walkway and went onto the crosswalk that would take them to the back of the building. Only it didn't happen that way, as it was Guy Jarrett calling out to

Gavin Brazelton.

"You, Brazelton, and you, elevate your hands!" Guy stepped away from the darker hulk of the large building behind him and farther into the openness of the yard.

The moment of shock past, Gavin Brazelton knew the Texan meant to gun him down. Before McLean, or even Jarrett knew his intentions, he'd jumped in behind McLean and wrapped a beefy arm around the man's neck as Gavin Brazelton groped for his shoulder holster. Out it came, and he yelled out at Guy Jarrett,

"You're awful stupid, Texas." He fired wildly at Jarrett still moving toward him, and he fired again, and missed.

In one fluid motion Guy brought the rifle to his shoulder, this without loosing stride. The stock of the Henry bucked against his shoulder, with flame spouting out of the barrel, and with the surrounding buildings throwing back the harsh crackling sound. Con McLean fully expected the slug to pierce into his chest, only it didn't happen that way. For the unerring aim of the Texan had caused the bullet to brush past McLean's face and hammer out one of Gavin Brazelton's eyes. The con man, petty thief, and murderer spilled down behind McLean, the handgun hitting the brick walkway to clatter away. The Texan's question of Con McLean wanting in on the action brought words gushing out of him as McLean brought his arms even higher.

"No . . . I don't want to die. The woman . . . they have her . . . the Brazeltons have her . . ."

"Hey, you?" someone shouted.

One of the guards appeared from around a building, and others, and Guy sprang toward the man standing by the body of Gavin Brazelton. "Quick,

207

where is she?"

"He . . . Mako has her. But he just left . . . for the Tenderloin Mine."

"Any horses back there?"

"Yes, my carriage." McLean hurried ahead of Guy Jarrett and they came around behind the building to find a saddled horse and one hitched to a carriage. Guy paused to go over and untie the reins and sent the horse galloping toward a star-lightened roadway, then he got into the carriage, and with Con McLean handling the reins, they headed out for the Tenderloin Mine.

"Her name is Reba Jo Cade."

"What? Oh, Cade, the woman from Texas. You're . . . Jarrett?"

"And you?"

"I, I handle the mining operations for Mr. Brazelton. I've pieced together some of what went on before, before I hired on here. I was . . ."

"Now I suppose you're going to tell me you were gonna quit," Guy said bitterly. "Mister, it just won't wash. For starters, why is he taking Reba Jo over to this mine?"

"To . . . to kill her."

Chapter Eighteen

On the way over to the Tenderloin Mine the way Mako Brazelton planned to kill Reba Jo was outlined to Guy Jarrett. Plying the reins, Con McLean rambled on about other misdeeds of Mako's. "Stealing ore from other mines was just the beginning. Can you imagine Mako Brazelton, this cheap thug, as a politician?"

"I know," responded Guy, "some politicians fittin' that bill, an' worse." After patting McLean down, a weapon Guy had come up with was a .32-caliber handgun. While bothering Guy was whether Mako Brazelton had heard that exchange of gunfire back at his smelter. Thus alerted that something had gone wrong, Mako could take Reba Jo some other place—out in the hills perhaps to kill her. "You say Mako worked her over pretty good. Didn't that bother you, McLean?"

"Had I interrupted they would have killed me. I . . . I suspect they were involved in that recent shooting. You know, as detailed in the newspapers."

"Heard all about some gunfighter and three others having themselves a gunfight. Brock Lacy was one of them."

"Yes, the outlaw. Lacy came out to see Mako at

the smelter with an 'or else' ultimatum."

"That or less got Brock Lacy killed. The way these Brazeltons work. How much farther?"

"Almost there—" McLean brought his running horse in a wide turn past some dark buildings, and then had it break stride when the street curled upward, "—just a few more blocks."

"Walk your hoss in from here," Guy told him. "What's the layout over there, any guards around?"

"I ordered the night shift to take the night off."

So's nobody'd get hurt when that dynamite was set off. More to cover up Mako's shady dealings down there."

They passed a row of shanties and tarpaper shacks to come upon the Tenderloin a little higher on the hill, and about a city block away. It was a small mining operation, the one gallows frame, trestles, slag heaps and a few unlighted buildings. Beyond this, on the upsloping hill, was the Neversweat, much larger and the workings of which Guy knew intimately. He'd quit—vowing not to go underground again. But to save the woman he loved he'd storm the gates of Hades, and it seemed tonight this was about to become grim reality.

Guy realized the wind had picked up, by the way it moaned in through the buildings and sent ore dust rising from slag heaps. Just ahead of them was the main entrance to the Tenderloin, with a guard by the closed gates, and Guy looked at McLean.

"Don't take me for somebody that gives a damn, you hear. When we get up there, you ask the guard if Brazelton arrived. He asks about me, tell him I'm another hard case you hired on." Guy eased out his Colt's and held it low at his side as their carriage slowed down by the gates.

"How's it going out here?"

"Oh, Mr. McLean? Awful quiet with nobody working tonight. And, yup, Mr. Brazelton just arrived."

McLean brought the carriage through the gate and up an incline of pebbly ground lined to their right by slag heaps and opposite a barnlike building. Farther along was a smaller building Guy took to be a doghouse or changing room for the miners. Unexpectedly the worn passageway dipped to reveal to Guy at least a half dozen men huddled between the two post gallows frame used to lower men and material into the mines and the engine room. Two of the men held lanterns, and then he saw Mako Brazelton coming out from behind the engine room building, him and another man and between them Reba Jo Cade.

He forgot about Con McLean seated with him in the carriage, that the man would cause any trouble, as all Guy could do was to stare at Reba Jo, to know for true she was still alive. Without warning, McLean made a grab for Guy's rifle, and they struggled for it, the horse bucked up but held there, and McLean shouted, "Its the Texan . . . help me . . ."

Guy managed to bring his Colt over and club McLean in the face, and the fight went out of McLean even as bullets began peppering toward the carriage. Somehow Guy scrambled the reins into his hands, and he lashed them out at the horse while at the same time wheeling the carriage around in a slewing angle. Then he jumped clear, with the barrage of leaden slugs still punching out at the carriage. He might have heard Con McLean screaming that he was hit, but all Guy wanted was to get free

211

of that gunfire, and then to go in and get Reba Jo.

Guy hit the ground at a run that carried him behind a slag heap, and he continued until he came around the high ore pile. He glimpsed Brazelton and another man forcing Reba Jo into the lower cage, two others climbing up to the higher of the two cages, and Guy headed that way even as the steel cage doors were slammed shut and the cages began descending into the mine.

Then he flopped down as the remaining three men spotted him. The Henry answered the guns of the hard cases, one of them folding over, the one in the middle, and now the one still alive suddenly realizing he'd better hightail it out of there or die. He broke away but too late, as a slug from Guy's Henry snapped in to break his backbone. Shoving up, Guy churned toward the engine room and entered it to shove the barrel of the Henry into the face of the engine room operator.

"What level are they at? Brazelton, what level?"

"Mis . . . please, I . . . nine hundred foot level . . ."

"What about that dynamite charge; whereabouts is it down there?"

"Guess its in that . . . that new tunnel the boys have been talking about. Get down there, head to your left down the main tunnel; someplace back there. Please . . . easy with that gun . . ."

"Listen good," drawled Guy Jarrett. "The rest of the police will be here most any time."

"Police?"

"That woman, she was kidnapped by Mako Brazelton. So unless you help me now you'll be on the old side of eighty before you get out of jail. Savvy? Bring up the cages; then I'm heading down. And

212

when Detective Elkington and his men get here, fill them in to what's happened."

"You betcha, mister," stammered the man as he threw some levers. "Kidnapped? That's serious business."

Guy, as he swung over and picked up a miner's helmet from a table, wished that right about now he had told the police he was going over to Mako Brazelton's smelter. As he knew that waiting down below would be the guns of Mako and his paid killers. With the cages ascending into view, he swung back and said,

"Stop it at the eight hundred foot level. Then when you hear my signal, bring the cages back up here. Just remember, you pull any double cross you could wind up like those lying dead just outside your doorway." He spun away and headed out to get into the lower cage, closed the door, and then he descended into the mine.

When he heard the sound of the cages being hoisted to the surface, Mako Brazelton swung around, the cap lamp attached to his helmet throwing inquisitive light back up the main tunnel. He'd left orders that the cages were to stay down here on the nine hundred foot level. "Damn," he said more to himself than the others, "I don't like this."

Of the three men with Mako, one was a hardrock miner, and who'd placed the dynamite charge. It was becoming clear to him that there was more involved here than his setting off the charge of dynamite. The woman looked in a bad way, had yet to say a word. Beat up as she was, and bound like that, he could only assume Brazelton's intentions for her. But he was unarmed, he knew that if he wanted to get out of this alive he'd have to play along.

"What do you think?"

One of the gunmen said to Mako, "They should have taken that Texan out."

"Yeah, what if they didn't. You keep watch back there. If it is the Texan coming down, kill the sonofabitch."

"Another thing to consider. Our only way out of here is them cages."

All of them except Reba Jo wore miner's helmets with cap lamps, and now there was a moment of uncertainty, especially for Mako Brazelton. This was his first time down in a copper mine. He felt boxed in, and if the Texan was up there, it would turn out to be a gun battle. His uneasiness was taken in by the hard cases. Now Reba Jo Cade saw her chance to add flame to their fears. The grip of Mako on her arm had loosened, and she broke away from him, stumbled backward and almost fell over the narrow gauge line over which ore carts were trundled.

"Yes, you're trapped," she said. "Did he ever tell you why he brought me down here? To leave me back there when that dynamite charge is set off. He'll kill me, he'll do the same to you . . . you fools . . ."

"You damned bitch!" flared Mako Brazelton. He started toward Reba Jo just as the miner spoke up.

"I sure as hell don't like this." He'd been one of those involved in working that pilfered ore out of the mine. Which hadn't bothered him all that much, as they'd received top wages. He had a family, too, a newborn baby and a wife about the same

214

age as the woman Brazelton was going to kill. He could sense the hired gunhands were having second thoughts, too, and he went on, "Ma'am, just what is going on here?"

Then Mako's gun belched flame to have the miner clutch at his belly, and Mako fired again to make sure the man wouldn't live. When the miner fell, his helmet dislodged from his head to douse the cap lamp. "Now, an extra thousand to you men once this is over."

"Yeah, a thousand . . . so what now . . . Mr. Brazelton . . ."

"Both of you over to the cage shaft. Signal to get them damned cages down here." He wheeled now on Reba Jo just starting to break away and thrust out a booted leg that sent her sprawling. Now he got her to her feet and rained curses at Reba Jo as they went together down the long main tunnel of the Tenderloin Mine.

Guy Jarrett knew the sound of the cages descending into the mine had reverberated down to the next level. He came out of the cage to let the metal door bang close behind him. The light from his helmet lamp picked out a scene still etched in his memory, that of a working copper mine. He knew sometimes just how confusing it can be to find one's way amongst the drifts, stopes and crosscuts. What he didn't know was of the difficulty being experienced by Mako Brazelton at the moment in finding the right crosscut to take Mako and his prisoner to that secret tunnel. Had he known, some of Guy's worries would have eased.

Born of necessity, and sheer desperation, was the

plan of Guy's to gain access to the next level down through one of the chutes, which were angling cuts into which ore was dropped. The length of the chute varied but as a rule continued downward for about a hundred feet, the distance between levels, the walls of the chute jagged so that if a man slipped he could get torn up bad or even killed. The other option of Guy's was to go down in the cages, which most certainly would see him killed outright.

"Either way, I'm coming for you, Mako."

Coming to the end of a crosscut it was here Guy saw the maw of a chute, the walls of the crosscut shored up with timbers as was the mouth of the chute, the narrow steel rails ending at the base of the rocky mine wall. He couldn't take the rifle as it would hinder his downward climb, but he took the time to lever out what shells it contained as they were calibered to be used in his Colt's. Discarding the. Henry, Guy crouched into the mouth of the chute, turned his head down some so's the cap lamp could shine along the angling and narrow chute walls, and he muttered edgily,

"Looks worse than I figured. But . . . here goes . . ."

By bracing himself, this by spreading out his legs and arms, he made slow downward progress, his boots seeking rocky protuberances as did his hands sometimes exposed to cutting rock edges. It was said that a man never sweated down in a mine. But the cold sweat of Guy's uncertainties gripped both his body and mind. A boot slipped, lodging him heavily against the right wall, and he almost lost his helmet. And for a moment he was certain he'd plunged down to slam into waste ore laying at the bottom of the chute.

Grimly he regained his composure, balance, went back to working downward. About halfway through the chute, he paused as he thought he heard Reba Jo crying out. Realized it was just his imagination. Then he pressed on, his outer garments covered with ore dusting and laced with cuts.

When Guy finally realized he was a mere few feet from the body of the chute, he let go to drop onto copper ore, and he slumped down. The chute, as he anticipated, had angled so that it came out someplace close to the vertical shaft where the cages were located, as the cages brought up both ore and miners. He struggled to his feet and moved out onto the crosscut floor. He held there and checked out the workings of his Colt's, to settle himself down.

"Three came down with Brazelton. Two gunmen, I reckon, one to set off the dynamite. Brazelton ain't the one to leave anything to chance. Which means he'll leave someone by the cage shaft."

Nearing the end of the crosscut, Guy put out the cap lamp before easing out into the main tunnel. Here he heard the murmur of voices, could make out the flashes of lights, and said, "Two of them; which evens the odds up considerable."

Now he went the other away along the tunnel, here and there shored up with thick beams. As he went, Guy considered the direction he was heading from the location of the cage shaft. He figured it to be to the east, which meant the tunnel they meant to dynamite had to be to his left, as to the north was located the Neversweat Mine. He passed some crosscuts, and then he slewed into one in his search for Reba Jo.

By sheer luck Mako Brazelton found a side tunnel that extended almost as long as the main tunnel and showed recent signs of ore having been taken out. He shoved Reba Jo ahead of him. It hadn't gone as he'd expected, and the foulness of his mood shone in his eyes. Turning his head so that the cap lamp splashed light upon the tunnel wall, he searched for the expected dynamite charge. But what Mako Brazelton didn't know was that dynamite had been placed in holes drilled along the tunnel wall. Deeper into the tunnel the fuses attached to the sticks of dynamite were longer, the hardrock miner shortening the fuses so that he'd light the longer one first and so work his way back to the mouth of the tunnel to light the last fuse, the shortest of all and a spitted or slow-burning fuse. An old hand at this, the hardrock miner knew that once the last fuse was set afire, it would give him just enough time to clear the tunnel, the chain of explosions that followed literally destroying the tunnel.

"Here we are," Mako exulted, "the dynamite charge." He smiled at the short length of dangling fuse and the round stick of dynamite lodged in the hole drilled in the wall.

Now he closed on Reba Jo, the smile still there, but thin and showing his nervousness at being down here. Still, he wanted to live up to the promise of his made back at his smelter. He grabbed Reba Jo and forced her down onto the tunnel floor, and she tried using her arms to fend him off. But he was too strong, as he kept on pawing at her clothing, his face contorted with lust and the need to have her.

Reba Jo screamed, "Damn you, you'll never have me."

"There ain't nobody here to save you, cowgirl."

He slapped out at her, to have her moan in pain, and laughed when she gave up the useless struggle. "That's better. Straddling her, he took off his helmet and set it down so that the light beamed toward them, and as he began doffing his coat, Reba Jo saw her chance.

She brought up a knee that struck him in the crotch, and Mako Brazelton doubled over in pain. She followed this by lashing out with her bound hands doubled into fists. The blow threw him to one side, with Reba Jo scrambling to her feet. She broke for the mouth of the tunnel, with Mako's voice raging out at her.

"You're dead . . . you damned hussy . . . dead . . ." He reached for his coat and managed to find his revolver.

Coming out of the tunnel into a crosscut, Reba Jo realized there was light where before it was only total blackness, and then it dawned on her that the light was coming from a miner's cap lamp, and she darted against the crosscut wall. She looked about for some weapon, bent to pick up a hunk of ore, only to have Guy Jarrett cry out, "Reba Jo? Look out . . . behind you!"

The gun of Mako Brazelton's sounded, the bullet chipping the wall near Reba Jo. Then the Colt's carried by Guy Jarrett answered, spouting flame again and again. Struck a couple of times, Mako spun back into the tunnel. This had all gone wrong, all because of that damned Texan. What's more, he couldn't believe he'd been hit. When he brought a hand away from his side it was wet with blood, his blood, and now the fear of all this took grip of Mako Brazelton.

"The dynamite . . . that's it . . . the fuses . . ."

Grimacing the pain away, he stumbled back to where he'd left his coat and the miner's helmet. Dropping to his knees, he fumbled out some wooden matches, struggled upright as he picked up the helmet and shoved it over his unkempt hair. There, a little bit deeper in the tunnel, one of the fuses. Now he struck a match to light it against the rock wall, and he brought the flaming end to the dangling fuse. There was a sputtering hiss as the fuse came alive, and only now did he realize just what he'd done. *Get out of here,* his mind screamed. Then he started at a weakening run for the mouth of the tunnel.

Too late he saw the light from the Texan's helmet lamp, but heedless of the bullets coming at him, Mako Brazelton fired his own gun as he kept moving, only he never got more'n a couple of more feet as the lone charge of dynamite exploded, churning out rocks and setting off other charges in a killing chain-reaction. The roof and side walls of the tunnel disintegrated into splintered rock and flying fragments that struck into the man trying to get away.

Out in the crosscut, Guy had managed to reach Reba Jo and bring her to the floor, where he huddled over her. The sound of exploding dynamite seemed to go on forever, as dust choked past to filled the crosscut and beyond. At last there were no more charges going off, and Guy's fear now was that the dynamite could have unleashed some underground pocket of gas, or weaken other parts of the mine.

"We've got to get out of here."

"Guy . . . Guy . . ." She buried her head in his chest and simply let the tears flow.

220

"Reba Jo . . . honey," he murmured, torn between taking her in his arms and never letting go and the immediate danger. He came to his knees and helped her rise. Then with his arm around her shaking shoulders, they started down the crosscut.

Somehow they made it back to the cage shaft, where, to Guy's surprise, the two men he'd spotted upon reaching the nine hundred foot level were gone. What he had expected was to gun it out with them. Now he looked upward upon hearing the humming of the cable lowering the cages back down into the mine. They couldn't stay here, he realized, and he brought Reba Jo back down the main tunnel and to a crosscut a short distance away. He fished out his pocket knife and pulled out one of the blades, and then Guy cut the ropes away from Reba Jo's wrists as he said, "Could be they went for reinforcements."

"At last . . . I can't believe at last I've found you."

"My fault as I should have worked with the police on this. But, glory, you look good." He swung out of the crosscut as the sound of the lowering cages grew louder, and then someone called out, "Reba Jo . . . Jarrett . . . can you hear me . . . ?"

She exclaimed, "Its Detective Elkington."

"You sure?"

"Spent enough time listening to his excuses." By his side Reba Jo moved back into the main tunnel and toward the cage shaft where men were emerging, the sweep of their lights taking in the dead body of the hardrock miner and the two survivors.

Wearily Guy explained just what had happened back in the deeper workings of the Tenderloin Mine. "There'll probably be nothing left of Brazelton to find." Only when they reached the surface and he was riding alongside Reba Jo in a carriage heading for the hospital did Guy Jarrett think of what he carried in his money belt. Unwrapping an arm from around the woman he loved snuggled in close, he pulled up his shirt and managed to open the money belt. From it he pulled out his abalone ring, and then to the surprise of Reba Jo Cade — once more dangling around her neck was the matching abalone pearl necklace.

"That necklace has been through hell."

"So have we."

"He sure enough worked you over."

She laughed, the timbre of her voice carrying a joyous happiness and the love she felt for this Texan. "Honey, you don't know the half of it."

"Guess I don't." There was a lingering kiss. "I expect we can just as well get hitched up here."

"Here, Mr. Jarrett, and pronto."

DANGER, SUSPENSE, INTRIGUE . . .
THE NOVELS OF

NOEL HYND

FALSE FLAGS	(2918-7, $4.50/$5.50)
THE KHRUSHCHEV OBJECTIVE	(2297-2, $4.50/$5.50)
REVENGE	(2529-7, $3.95/$4.95)
THE SANDLER INQUIRY	(3070-3, $4.50/$5.50)
TRUMAN'S SPY	(3309-5, $4.95/$5.95)

Available wherever paperbacks are sold, or order direct from the Publisher. Send cover price plus 50¢ per copy for mailing and handling to Zebra Books, Dept. 4033, 475 Park Avenue South, New York, N.Y. 10016. Residents of New York and Tennessee must include sales tax. DO NOT SEND CASH. For a free Zebra/ Pinnacle catalog please write to the above address.

BENEATH THE CALM OF THE DEEP,
BLUE SEA, HEART-POUNDING DANGER AWAITS

DEPTH FORCE

THE ACTION SERIES BY

IRVING A. GREENFIELD

#4: BATTLE STATIONS	(1627-1, $2.50/$3.50)
#5: TORPEDO TOMB	(1769-3, $2.50/$3.50)
#9: DEATH CRUISE	(2459-2, $2.50/$3.50)
#10: ICE ISLAND	(2535-1, $2.95/$3.95)
#11: HARBOR OF DOOM	(2628-5, $2.95/$3.95)
#12: WARMONGER	(2737-0, $2.95/$3.95)
#13: DEEP RESCUE	(3239-0, $3.50/$4.50)
#14: TORPEDO TREASURE	(3422-9, $3.50/$4.50)

Available wherever paperbacks are sold, or order direct from the Publisher. Send cover price plus 50¢ per copy for mailing and handling to Zebra Books, Dept. 4033, 475 Park Avenue South, New York, N.Y. 10016. Residents of New York and Tennessee must include sales tax. DO NOT SEND CASH. For a free Zebra/Pinnacle catalog please write to the above address.